fast break

LACROSSE MY HEART
BOOK 2

CATE TAYLER

ELEPHANT SHOES PRESS

For Larisa and Moira, my darling girls. I've loved watching you play your hearts out on the field, but even more, I've loved watching the beautiful, fierce young women you have become.

author's note

If you are at all familiar with women's lacrosse, or if you feel inspired to check out some games after reading the Lacrosse My Heart series, I feel I should warn you: Professional women's lacrosse as I've described it in my books does not exist in reality. I've taken many liberties with how the fictional league in my stories is organized and operates, because frankly, women's sports still don't receive the respect and attention they should. Lacrosse is a popular sport for men and women, but even men's lacrosse is not broadcast on a scale anywhere near the other major sports. So you can imagine how the women fare!

I am a lacrosse mama. All four of my children played. My oldest daughter took her sticks with her to college, and my youngest daughter, at the time of this writing, is the goalie for her high school JV team. I wrote these stories featuring women players because I wanted to create a world for them where their hard work, talent, and love for the game were represented on par with any other major sport.

So please forgive me if I've set you up with any unrealistic expectations. There is no major multi-level stadium. The current professional league for women, Women's Lacrosse League (WLL), is brand new as of 2025 and comprises only five East Coast teams that play in the winter. It didn't really serve the story I wanted to tell. I had fun creating a new world for my characters, who in my head are all bad asses like my daughters. I hope I translated that well on the page.

Enjoy the story! And if you haven't had an opportunity to catch a women's lacrosse game (professional or college), make a plan to do so when the next season rolls around!

Cate

June 2025

ONE

palmer

I'M HAVING A SHITTY PRACTICE.

I know it. The team knows it. Worst of all, Coach Arkhady knows it. This is my chance to prove I'm ready to start in the Baltimore Battle's first game of the season against the Syracuse Warriors. Tisha Baker, the team's starting goalie and my mentor, had injured her knee pre-season, and the starting position is open. She's retiring at the end of the season, and she'd recommended me as her replacement. Only if I keep playing like this, I'll be lucky they don't trade me. I can't bring myself to look over at the sidelines and see Tisha's disappointment.

"C'mon, York," Coach Arkhady shouts. "Pay attention out there."

I jerk my head in acknowledgment and take a defensive stance in the goal. We're playing a half-field scrimmage meant to test the defense, with the attackers wearing blue pennies. As the play unfolds midfield with a successful defense, my mind once again drifts to last night's humiliation. All I can see is Brennan's smarmy face telling me he's engaged, while his intended–who happens to be my cousin, Rania–sits next to him with a serene, Cheshire-cat smile.

A fresh wave of rage surges through me, distracting me from the play. I'm not quick enough to switch my stick to the other post and take a shot right to my thigh. Below the padded shorts, of course.

"Son of a—"

"Sorry, Palmer," Jewel says.

"My bad," I groan, scooping the ball and flipping it to her.

My teammates reset at the centerline for the draw, one of the offensive coaches holding the mesh of their sticks together with the ball between them. He steps back and blows his whistle. The ball pops up and one of the attackers bats it out of the air toward Jewel.

"Clear your mind." I grip my stick with both hands and crouch in front of the goal. Jewel runs toward me, dodging first one, then two defenders. She makes a quick pass to Allie, who performs her signature spin move, positioning her for a perfect shot.

"Crash!" I yell at the defense, but I'm a beat off and they don't move in time to stop Allie, who launches a perfect shot over my left shoulder and into the net.

"Fuck." I smack the post with my stick.

"All right, water break," one of the other coaches calls out. I take off my gloves and unclip my helmet, limping off the field. I rub at the spot where Jewel's shot hit.

"That's gonna be some bruise," Tisha says, handing me a water bottle.

I take it and squeeze the contents into my mouth, then slump onto the bench. "I deserve it. I suck out there."

"Yeah, I noticed." Tisha adjusts her knee brace. "Wanna talk about it?"

"Not particularly."

"But you will. Because it's me." Tisha flashes a too-large grin and bats her thick false lashes, their glittery edges catching the sunlight. I laugh in spite of myself.

"Brennan stopped by last night." Recalling last night's confrontation made the water bitter.

"Please tell me he begged you to take him back and you kicked his sorry ass to the curb," Tisha says. She hadn't ever liked Brennan, but when he dumped me the day after New Year's four months ago, she'd gone full-on scorched earth when it came to him. I had to physically restrain her from pushing him off the balcony when he moved out of our apartment.

"Hah. Nothing so satisfying. No, he wanted to tell me to my face that he is getting married in August. He even brought his fiancée with him so they could tell me together."

"What kind of sadistic dick drip thinks it's appropriate to bring your future bride to meet your ex? Why would he think you'd give a shit who or what he's marrying? That's some self-important bullshit right there."

I twist my lips. "They didn't want me to hear about it from the rest of my family, since the woman he's marrying is—drumroll, please—my cousin, Rania."

Tisha's mouth drops open. I gesture at her face. "Yeah, that was my reaction at first."

She slowly shakes her head. "I'm stunned. What is wrong with your cousin?"

"Oh, plenty," I snort. "I mean, she's perfect on the surface. Literally, she's a beauty queen and graduated top of her class at Vassar, and is now some junior associate at a big deal financial firm. She's the daughter my parents wish they had."

"After this, I doubt your perfect little cousin will still be favored over you."

"You don't know my parents," I grouse. I'm not exaggerating. Rania and I are the same age, so my entire life has been one comparison after another, with me consistently falling short. Except for sports. Rania may have been the more graceful dancer, but she could no more throw, kick, hit, or bat a ball than I could plié without falling over. Of course, in my parents' world, that still put her ahead of me since women in our social sphere didn't compete in men's games.

Tisha turns to face me. "Okay. So now we know what's wrong. How do we fix it so you don't lose your starting spot to Jackie? I love the girl and she's got game, but this is your time. You know I back you a hundred percent."

I blow out a breath. This is Tisha my mentor speaking, narrowing in on my weaknesses and finding a way to turn them into strengths. Unfortunately, this isn't something she can drill out of me, and I tell her as much. She dismisses my comment with a wave of her hand. "Bull. This is a crisis of confidence. You're letting that worm into your head."

"I can't believe I actually thought he was going to propose to me," I scoff. "Instead of an engagement ring for Christmas, I get a 'You care more about your lacrosse career than our future' lecture and boom—five months later, he's marrying my cousin. He knew Rania and I despised each other. How much she tortured me." I don't voice my suspicion about this thing with Rania being a catalyst for our breakup all those months ago. I don't want to know if it's true because I can't afford to lose another scrap of dignity.

"That's what I'm saying, Boo. Don't let that piece of crap and his skank ruin this for you. Like I told you, any man who's threatened by your success is no man at all. There's nothing wrong with putting your career first. Men do it all the time. How do you think I've gotten to the top of my game? Or Ava? Or Coach, for that matter? We're women playing in what used to be solely a man's game. Women's Major League Lacrosse couldn't exist without women like us putting our hearts and souls into it. Brennan should've been proud of his girl. He isn't worth screwing up your game for."

I'd met Brennan Hank three years ago, shortly after the Philadelphia team I'd been warming the bench for had traded me to the Baltimore Battle. At first, he seemed impressed that I was a pro athlete. Things changed after we moved in together. His support waned until it was all but non-existent. It should've been my first clue he wasn't the right one for me, but my parents adored him, and on paper, he was everything you could ask for in a mate. I assumed he'd come around, especially as I started to find more playing time and more success. Instead, he dumped me.

And now he is marrying my rival.

"The first game of the season is tomorrow. If you keep practicing like shit, Coach'll put Jackie in as my replacement instead of you. You really want that ass to cost you a starting position?"

I breathe deep and exhale slowly. This is the proverbial smack upside the head I need. "Okay. I'll forget about Brennan and focus on the rest of this season." I squeeze the water bottle into my mouth.

"That's my girl." Tisha taps her lips. "You know what else you need? You need a confidence boost. You need to get laid."

I choke, coughing up some of the water I accidentally inhaled instead of swallowing. This drew the attention of my teammates and some of the coaches. Tisha pats me on the back. "She's okay. Wrong pipe."

"But we're gonna find you the right one," she mutters under her breath.

"T," I splutter, "are you serious right now?"

"As a heart attack." She thumps my back one more time. "You've been a dry spell for too long and this ain't helping. Orgasms equal endorphins. Endorphins equal stress relief and happy thoughts. Less stress combined with happy thoughts equals better playing. I'm going to write a book about it someday."

I laugh, not entirely sure she's kidding. "And how do you propose I do that?"

"Let me think about it. Meanwhile, Coach is getting ready to blow her whistle. You gonna go out there and slay?"

I swipe the back of my hand across my mouth, grab my helmet and gloves, and stand. "Watch me."

TWO

palmer

PRACTICE WENT BETTER after Tisha's pep talk and Coach announced I'd be starting in our first game. After showering and dressing, I leave the locker room and take the elevators to the executive offices. Coach sent me upstairs to the media suite, where the communications team would be putting together a promotional feature introducing me as the starting goalie. I never liked being the center of attention, but the Director of Marketing is married to our team captain, Ava, and my friend, Charlie, is the Director of Digital Media. I'm in good hands.

Still, I use the reflective surface of the elevator doors as a mirror to double-check the powder and lip gloss Jewel helped me with. I smooth down the strands of my blonde bob, wishing for the hundredth time I'd gotten pink highlights. When I mentioned to Brennan I wanted to put colorful streaks in my hair, he dismissed it as childish. "Imagine what your parents would say," he'd said after I showed him a few examples. He was right; my parents wouldn't like it, but there was little I could do that they would approve of.

Speaking of—my phone jingles with the Imperial March

from Star Wars. "MOM" flashes on the screen as the elevator arrives at the third floor and the doors slide open. "Hi, Mom."

"Why didn't you call us?" my mother demands. Elaine York was never one for the usual pleasantries, at least not when it came to her only daughter. "I had to hear from Aunt Dora that Rania is engaged to Brennan."

I draw in a breath. "I only found out last night."

"This will be awkward," she sighs. "What will people say?"

The ball I took to my leg earlier today is nothing compared to the kick my mother delivers to my stomach. Of course, her first thought isn't about my well-being. I shouldn't be surprised, and I'm not, but I can't help the hurt. "Thanks, Mom, I'm doing okay. The news was shocking, but it doesn't matter in the grand scheme of things."

"It matters to us," my mother continues, either ignorant or oblivious to my sarcasm. "This family has never been a topic of gossip before, and I don't intend for that to change now."

"It's not like I can control what Brennan and Rania do, Mom. This isn't my fault."

"I know that," she says. "But, you can control your reaction and how this affects our family."

"Yeah? How?"

"I'm not condoning what Rania did," my mother continues. "But she is family, and like it or not, Brennan will be, too. If you can move past the—"

"Awkwardness?" I scoff. "You want me to pretend everything is okay."

"Are you still in love with him?"

I gagged. "God, no."

"Then what will it hurt? Please, Palmer. Is it too much to ask you to take the high road here?"

I hold back a grunt. "Fine, Mom. Whatever."

"Thank you."

"I have to go, but I did want to share some good news," I say, injecting false lightness into my voice. "I'm the starting goalie in tomorrow's game. Will you and Dad be able to come?"

"I'm afraid not. We're entertaining a new client and his wife tomorrow for dinner," she says. "Maybe next time."

It's an empty promise. They've yet to come to one of my professional games and have only watched one or two of my college performances. My mother saw this as an indulgence, a hobby. Not a true career and calling. She'd never respect what I do, and her next words confirm her feelings.

"Honestly, Palmer. This should be a wake-up call. You're not getting any younger. How much longer are you going to keep playing games? You're twenty-seven. You should come home, use that expensive degree we paid for, and join your father's firm. I promise you'll find the right man to settle down with."

"You mean someone you and Dad pick out for me?"

"Could we do any worse than you have?" She sighs. "I don't mean to be harsh, Palmer. I'm only looking out for you."

"Right." I clear my throat, my face stinging from being slapped in the face with my past mistakes. "I have to go. Talk to you later."

My throat burns as I turn off my phone. I breathe slow and deep until my emotions are under control. My mother is right; I can't control what someone else does, but I can control how I react. Unfortunately, I can't seem to control my wish to be the daughter they want.

There's a flurry of activity going on in the media office when I arrive. Liberty, who handles press relations, has her phone pressed between her ear and shoulder while she furiously types on the laptop in front of her. Mei, in charge of player-fan relations, is talking to Dante, the events coordinator, while he writes on a giant whiteboard. And a few interns are setting up ring lights and a stool in the corner where a Maryland flag hangs as a backdrop.

I look for Charlie, who was one of the first friends I made when I moved to Baltimore. The first time I met him, he put me at ease with his flirty jokes and easy charm. My stomach had done a little flip when Charlie smiled at me, dimples bracketing luscious lips. Lean and broad-shouldered, with dark brown, wavy hair cut long and coppery-brown eyes that perpetually gleamed with mischief, he was without question the hottest man in the city of Baltimore. Hell, the entire world. And when the world included Chris Hemsworth and Michael B. Jordan, that was saying something. Too bad I had just started dating Brennan, who at the time seemed like the safer choice. What a sucker I was.

Charlie has heartbreaker written all over him, and from his reputation, my first impression wasn't far off. I'm sure I wouldn't have had a chance with him, anyway. The women he dated seemed to be my physical opposites. I'm fit and happy with my body, but I'm also realistic. Charlie prefers petite waifs. At 5'11", I'm the tallest player on the team and often the tallest person in the room, except when Charlie is around. He's half a head taller than me, unlike Brennan, who was barely taller and only when his loafer had a heel on it.

I don't want to think about Brennan anymore. So I focus on Charlie. He's wearing a fitted button-down, crisp white with the Battle logo on the pocket and sleeves rolled up to his elbows. His forearms are like catnip. Golden olive skin, dusted with dark hair and defined by thick, ropy muscles. *He must do a lot of pull-ups.*

"Palmer York," he says, jarring me out of my thoughts. "Here you are."

I spread my hands. "Here I am."

He sweeps my body with a glance and gives me a dimpled smile. "Congratulations on the starting slot. It's well deserved."

"Thanks."

Charlie guides me to the setup in the corner where the interns are. "This is Emma and Benji. We're going to ask some get-to-know-you questions. Then we'll talk about your progression from college player to your first team and how their loss became our gain when they traded you. We'll do our best not to puke when we talk about Philly."

I laugh. My former team, the Philadelphia Stars, is our biggest rival. Charlie attaches the lavaliere mic to my collar and adjusts the wire, his fingers tickling the skin of my collarbone. "We'll prompt you with questions you can answer naturally, like we're sitting in your kitchen shooting the shit. Except you'll be looking into the camera." I nod in understanding.

"Try to repeat the question in your answer. First one," Emma says, holding an index card. "Tell us a little about where you're from and about your family."

I straighten and look into the lens. "I'm from Frederick County, about an hour west of Baltimore. My dad is a real estate developer, and my mom serves on the boards of several charities. I'm an only child, but I have had nearly every pet under the sun, so I always had a playmate."

"Did you play youth lacrosse?"

"Oddly enough, I didn't play lacrosse when I was younger. I danced for a number of years. My mom wanted me to be a ballerina. But by the time I was eight, it was clear I wasn't cut out to do pointe. Sorry, Mom!" I delight when the team snickers at my joke and start to relax.

"So when did you first pick up a stick?"

"My high school had a team and I thought, why not? It looked interesting. I wasn't much into running, so I liked the idea of being a goalie."

Once I go over my bio and answer questions about life as a Battle goalie, Emma thanks me. She unclips the mic and I stand.

"Is that it?" I ask, surprised at how quick this was.

Charlie scribbles something on a clipboard and hands it to Benji. "For tonight. We'll take photos of you tomorrow in uniform, both pre- and post-game. Of course, we're always getting on-field action during the game."

"Okay."

"I'll walk you out." Charlie puts a hand on the small of my back and leads me back through the maze of desks. He holds the door open for me and follows me to the elevator bank.

"Are you excited about the game?" he asks.

"Nervous might be a better description," I reply. "I'm afraid of letting the team down. Tisha leaves behind big shoes to fill."

He moves his arm to my shoulders and squeezes, enveloping me in his familiar woodsy scent. "You're going to be great. You're a rock star out there and Coach Arkhady wouldn't have selected you to take Tisha's place if she didn't believe in you."

"Thank you," I say, giving him a grateful smile. "It's nice to hear it."

"It happens to be true." He releases me and punches the down button for the elevators. "Listen, a few of us are meeting for happy hour at Poe's. Let off some steam before the big start of the season tomorrow. You should join us. Unless you have plans?"

"I don't, but," I wrinkle my nose, "Coach wants us tucked in early tonight so we're not wasted for the game."

"Showtime is noon tomorrow, right? I promise to have you in bed before ten."

His eyes glint with mischief and his gaze once again wanders over my body. Am I imagining it, or did his voice get deeper? A little shiver skittered up my spine. He's always been playful and a little flirty; it's who he is. This is different, and I'm not sure why. Probably because I have Tisha's suggestion about getting laid running through my head.

"I'll think about it," I finally respond. The bell chimes as the car arrives, and I hurry on as soon as the doors open, eager to move out of his orbit.

"I'll keep an eye out for you." He holds my gaze, his dimples deepening as his smile grows wider just before the doors close, leaving me alone—and inexplicably edgy.

THREE

palmer

I ENTERTAIN the thought of going out for the length of the ride to the lobby. Once there, reality sets in. I have no business going out to a bar the night before a game. Some of my teammates are going out to "blow off steam," like Charlie said, but they're hitting up a club and those who aren't are spending the evening with their families or significant others. I didn't want to go dancing, and I no longer had a significant other, which left a quiet night at home in my apartment, going over game film or—more likely—binge watching the latest season of Reacher. The last thing I want to do is go out and having to pretend everything is okay. Other than Tisha, no one in the organization knows about Brennan and Rania, and I plan to keep it that way. No one cares about or needs to know the sordid details of my pathetic love life. A pang of loneliness shoots through my chest as I unlock the door and enter the silent apartment.

It's a swanky place. One bedroom, one-and-a-half bath, in the tony Roland Park neighborhood of Baltimore, with a private garage and pool. The stainless steel appliances were all new and the ensuite bathroom boasts a soaking tub, which my aching muscles love. I'd rather live closer to the stadium or nearer my teammates, but my parents insisted, and Brennan was all too eager to take them up on their offer to cover first and last month's rent when we moved in. I considered moving when the lease is up in the fall, but I'd really miss the tub.

When Brennan moved out, he left behind the furniture but also empty bookshelves and cabinets, and voids on the wall where art once hung. I haven't gotten around to replacing anything he took, so after five months, the place looks only half-lived in. Maybe it's time I restock the bookshelves and buy new sets of dishes. It'd been our apartment for so long, but it's time I make it mine and mine alone.

I drop my bag by the bedroom door and toe off my sneakers, then collapse onto the double bed we'd once shared. I stare up at the painting hanging above the headboard, a sensual abstract piece by Cameron Blake, the major league ballplayer-turned-artist of a woman emerging from a daisy. It had cost a small fortune, one of the few times I indulged myself and refused to give in to Brennan's derision of my taste.

It's quiet, except for the occasional horn and the low bass thrum from my neighbor's radio. Too quiet. I turn my face into my pillow and stare at the empty side of the bed. The sheets are cool to touch, a feature I usually appreciate. Other than during my time in Philly, when I didn't have time or inclination to date, this is the longest I've been without a steady boyfriend since high school. I didn't have many relationships, but each one, including Brennan, was a serious relationship.

There was Barry, my freshman-year boyfriend. He was a junior and tutored me in statistics and probability the first semester. We had our first date after finals, and by the end of the year, I'd moved my things into his off-campus apartment.

Things were great until he came back from Spring Break with a pierced ear and a sorority girl named Darby.

Next came Alexei, the right wing for our school's hockey team. I spent all of junior year and the start of senior year walking on clouds as his girl. Right until I walked in on him taking a shot on the five-hole with his roommate's girlfriend. His roommate, Ignacio, and I trauma bonded over the situation, and by May, when I was drafted to play for Philadelphia after graduation, I was already planning my wedding to Ig around the season. Instead of proposing to me, however, he eloped with said former girlfriend.

Then there's Brennan. Another three years wasted because I'm so stupid with my heart. What do I have to show for it? This aching loneliness and a cold bed. I pound the mattress, disgusted with myself, and scoop up my phone to text Tisha.

ME

I figured out my problem. I need a fling.

TISHA

Yeahhh... that's what I told you

ME

No, you said I needed to get laid. But I need more. I fall in love with the guys I date wayyyy too quickly. Do you know I have never gone to bed with someone I wasn't in a committed relationship with? I'm a serial monogamist and I must be stopped! 😱

TISHA

😊 Girl, how much you have to drink already?

ME

Nothing. I'm sitting here wallowing in self-pity, thinking about my previous relationships.
Each one burned hot and fast, like a shooting star, until it fizzled out when they found someone else.

TISHA

You're losing me... What are you saying exactly? 😕

ME

I'm saying I need to change my attitude. No more falling in love, at least not at first sight.

TISHA

Alright... but how?

ME

Like you said. Get laid. It'll be like a vaccine. Once I prove to myself I can have a fling with a guy–date him, duck him–with no hearts involved, then the next time I meet someone with potential, I'll know how to keep it casual until I'm absolutely sure. My brain won't hang out the "Committed" sign at the first organism.

ME

*fuck *orgasm 😬

TISHA

Maybe I've had too much to drink because that's making sense 😵

ME

I'm going to be seeing Brennan and Rania at all major family events, and minor ones, too, if my mother has any say. I can't face them when I'm so lonely and I definitely can't face them with another failed relationship. The next time I fall in love, it has to be the last time.

TISHA

So you think this will work? You think getting some good 🍆 will change your brain chemistry?

ME

Crude. But accurate.

> **TISHA**
>
> Got anyone in mind?

> **ME**
>
> Charlie Salinas invited me to join the media team for happy hour at Poe's.

The text bubbles bounce for half a minute.

> **TISHA**
>
> Charming Charlie??? Girl, you have my blessing 🙌 🔥 🔥 🔥

> **ME**
>
> I'm not his usual type. He likes pixie women.

> **TISHA**
>
> So? Show him what it's like to be with a real woman 🍑

I grin at Tisha's confidence in me.

> **ME**
>
> Might be a problem—I'm not exactly experienced. My body count is single digit, and never anything more adventurous than me on my knees. Especially Brennan.

> **TISHA**
>
> Enough. Don't need to hear it.
> 🙄 But Charlie is a great choice because he's so experienced. I bet he can teach you things... And he's hot AF

> **ME**
>
> So. We're agreed. I'm going to go out and hit on Charlie.

> **TISHA**
>
> If you're looking for a good time, then go. Just don't forget we have a game tomorrow night.

I'll be home early, mom. Tonight is more like scouting, feeling him out. Nothing would be more mortifying than getting rejected by Charming Charlie.

I put my phone on the charger and sigh. I've never had a one-night stand or short-term fling before. I'm not usually confident enough to pick up an attractive guy in a bar and take him back to my bed, not that there have been all that many opportunities. I've never wanted to do anything to tarnish my reputation or my family's. I've never done anything so recklessly *fun*.

"Let's do it." Mind made up, I push off the bed. Charlie and I have been friends since I joined the team and he's always been a little flirtatious. It's his personality. Friends with benefits is something I've never tried before, and Charlie strikes me as the perfect candidate. But would he be interested? I'll never know unless I put myself out there. I am going to be spontaneous and bubbly and fun. *Suck on that, Brennan.*

Too bad my closet doesn't reflect my new attitude. Other than athleisure or jeans and tees, I have the more formal clothes my mother insisted on buying me. If I were going to a tea party or a ladies' garden club meeting, I'd have a wealth of outfits to choose from. What my mother's obsession with florals is I will never understand, but it's one of our major disconnects. She is into frilly, flowery, and feminine; I pref sporty, comfortable, and functional, an aesthethic now biting me in the ass.

I flip through my hangers, finally pulling out a silky turquoise cap-sleeved v-neck to pair with my black denim capris. The rouching under the bosom emphasizes my larger-than-average chest, so I don't wear this shirt often. Tonight it would be a bonus to catching Charlie's attention. I rub my favorite peach and wild berry moisturizer into my skin and dress, relieved nothing is too tight.

There isn't much I can do with my hair, so I leave it down, but I pay a little more attention to my makeup using a trick I'd learned on TikTok to make my eyes stand out. After adding a pair of silver dangles and a chunky strand of multicolored beads, I give myself one more check in the mirror. I hum an old Springsteen song as I slick on a peony pink lip gloss. "Well," I tell my reflection, "We ain't a beauty but we're all right."

FOUR

palmer

THIRTY MINUTES LATER, my confidence wobbles and anxiety ratchets to its highest level. I survey the scene inside Poe's, a small bar in the Federal Hill neighborhood of Baltimore and a short Lyft ride from the apartment. It's a favorite hangout of the team, and I've been here before, but suddenly I'm overwhelmed. I spot Charlie at the bar talking to an attractive brunette, another pixie. She wears a short skirt that rides up to expose flawless thighs and a shimmery red halter top that pops against bronzed skin similar to Charlie's, only hers has the orangey undertone you get from badly applied spray tans.

She's talking, constantly reaching out to touch him, while he appears to be listening intently. Guess Charlie already found his girl for the night. I debate turning around and leaving before anyone notices me, but I hesitate a second too long.

"Palmer!" Emma, the intern I met earlier, waves me over to a tall top table where she sits with Benji, Liberty, Dante, Mei, and a woman I don't recognize. They greet me with a cheer. Dante lifts his bottle of beer in a salute.

"Keep!" he shouts. I duck my head, imagining all the heads in the bar turning toward me.

"Keep?" asks the puzzled woman standing next to Mei. "Keep what?"

Dante laughs. "It's her position. She's the goalkeeper. The 'Keep'."

"Don't worry, sweetie," Mei says. "Keep hanging with me, you'll catch on."

"Most people call me Palmer," I say, scooting onto an empty stool between Dante and Mei.

"This is my girlfriend, Francesca," Mei says, draping an arm around the brunette's shoulders. "She just moved here from Indiana and she knows nothing about sports."

"And how much do you know about playing multiple voices in a single concerto?" Francesca counters, sticking her tongue out at Mei.

"You got me there." Mei squeezes Francesca's shoulder and lets her arm drop. She explains, "Chessie's a concert pianist. She's auditioning for the BSO."

"Oh, I love the Baltimore Symphony Orchestra," I exclaim. "Good luck, er, break a leg?"

"I'll take either," Chessie laughs.

"What are you having?" Dante asks. He gestures to the bar. "Let me get you the first round to congratulate you."

My gaze drifts to Charlie again. The woman is still talking and now leans into him, a hand on his chest. A flash of jealousy turns into dismay. This was a stupid idea. I should take his interest in this other woman as a sign.

"Um," I look away before anyone can tell I'm staring at Charlie and point at the bottle Dante holds. "How about whatever you're having. I can't stay long. Big day tomorrow."

"Be right back. Anyone else?" Dante takes refill orders and goes to the bar.

"Anyone else from the team coming?" Liberty says, flipping her glossy red ponytail over her shoulder. She looks past me, her eyes narrowing. Is she glaring at Dante or Charlie, or someone else entirely? My money is on Charlie.

"Just me tonight." I try to sound nonchalant. "Didn't want to go clubbing but too wired to stay home, you know?"

We talk for a few minutes about our prospects for the season, how the new offensive coordinator is doing, and whether we'd do better than our brother Red Hawks this year. Liberty's attention keeps straying toward the bar, and a pang of pity for her tweaks in my chest if it's Charlie she's so interested in. I want to hop into bed with him, sure, but I know better than to expect anything more. Which is why Charlie is the perfect candidate for my little experiment.

A cold bottle appears in front of me. I look up to thank Dante and come face-to-face with Charlie instead. He treats me to a two-dimple smile. "You came."

"I did," I reply, my heart leaping in my chest. *Calm. Down.*

Charlie squeezes in between Dante and me. "I'm glad."

My cheeks must be turning bright pink, but I keep my response nonchalant. "Me, too."

Dante delivers the other drinks and the conversation resumes. It's not long before I am so at ease, I haven't had time to think about Brennan or the real reason I came out tonight. Charlie walks to the bar as the conversation turns into a spirited debate over whether TikTok challenges were lame or prime publicity opportunities. He returns with two fresh beers and sets one down in front of me.

"Excited about tomorrow?" he asks, leaning against the table to face me.

"Nervous is more like it," I say, taking a sip of the hoppy brew. "Practice wasn't the greatest today."

Charlie shrugs. "You were just getting the yips out. Tomorrow will be better."

He bends his head closer to mine. "You'll be great, I know it."

His voice is liquid velvet, his breath hot on my neck. Desire sparks in me and the flame settles low in my belly. My lips part. His face is close enough, if I turn my head to the right, our lips would nearly touch. I keep my head down and pick at the corner of the label. "You think so?"

"I know so. You've got the moves, York." His voice is practically a purr in my ear. Every nerve in my body stands at attention. My plan for this evening is back on the table.

I'm jerked back to the present by the clatter of a glass being put down—hard—on the table. Charlie straightens, the sudden space between us doing little to cool my heated body. Liberty stares at Charlie with undisguised contempt.

"Where's your little fan from earlier, Charlie?" she sneers.

Charlie's lips flatten. "If you mean the woman I was talking to, I imagine she joined up with her friends."

"Got her number in your pocket for later?" Liberty's words have a bite to them, evident to everyone considering their embarrassed glances at one another.

"Not your business, is it?" Charlie offers a tight smile.

"Guess not," Liberty says. She grabs her wristlet off the tablet. "Well, it's been fun, but even though showtime for the players isn't until noon," she stares pointedly at me, and I take another drink to hide my discomfort, "I need to be in by nine. It's going to be a long day."

Mei checks her phone. "I think Chessie and I are going to head out, too. She has rehearsal early in the morning. We'll walk with you."

"It was nice meeting you all," Chessie says, taking Mei's hand.

Emma slides off her stool. "I think I'm going to call it, too."

She gives me a quick hug and leaves with Benji, leaving Dante, Charlie, and me.

"I thought things were better between you and Liberty," Dante says once everyone else has gone.

Charlie glances sideways at me before answering him. I sip my beer and pretend disinterest, though I'm dying to know more.

"It goes in waves. Some days, I think we can be friends, and then there are times like tonight." Charlie shakes his head and finishes his beer.

Dante nods his chin at me. "Charlie and Liberty hooked up when he first started here."

"Dante," Charlie winces.

"What? Everyone else knows. Anyway," Dante continues to explain to me. "They hooked up. Didn't end well. Ever since, Liberty's made it her mission to be a bitch to Charlie every chance she gets."

"Hey, don't call her that," Charlie says curtly. "I hurt her feelings. I deserve whatever she dishes out. I take full responsibility."

"She needs to get over it."

"Can we drop it?" Charlie darts another glance at me, then gives Dante a peeved look. "Please?"

"Okay." Dante raises his hands, palms out. "This old man needs to head home. Lucia is probably wondering where the hell I am."

"Lucia your girlfriend?" I ask, leaning into the topic change.

"My cat," Dante announces proudly. He opens his phone and taps the screen a few times, then turns it around to show me the prettiest Calico. "The only pussy that hasn't let me down."

I choked on my last swallow of beer. Charlie slaps Dante upside the head. "There's a lady present, moron."

Dante's face flushes bright red. "Sorry, Palmer. I think I had one too many tonight."

I bite back a grin. "It's okay, Dante. See you tomorrow."

"Good luck out there," he says in parting.

The woman in red is at the bar again, casting annoyed glances our way. Charlie nods at my half-drunk beer. "Another?"

I wave him off, my confidence draining. The woman in red is hot and obviously very interested. I'm not about to cock-block my friend. "No. I should get home. Make sure I'm mentally prepared for tomorrow."

Charlie checks his watch. "It's barely past nine. Want some ice cream? There's a great little shop around the corner. Or do you want something to eat other than pub food?" He gestures to the empty baskets that had held an assortment of fried appetizers we'd all picked on.

I hesitate, but Tisha's voice rings in my head. I'm still not sure I can go through with the plan, but for now it's just ice cream. I nod. "Sure. Ice cream sounds delicious."

FIVE

charlie

SHE SHOWED UP. Palmer York fucking showed up.

I have had a crush on this woman since I met her three years ago. I once pointed her out to my brother and he didn't understand. "Kind of big boned, isn't she?" he'd said.

I punched him.

Not hard, just enough so he knew not to talk about her like that again. As far as I'm concerned, she's gorgeous. Tall, only a few inches shorter than me, with strong arms and muscled legs. How many nights have I fantasized about having those legs squeezing the life out of me while I pumped inside her? Too many to count.

And now here she is, and we're getting ice cream.

It's not solely about her looks, though her unusual eyes—aquamarine with a deep gold ring around the center—were enough to stop a man in his tracks. She's smart, kind, funny as hell. But of course, the first woman to catch my eye in over ten years would have a boyfriend.

Crazy to be hung up on this one woman, right? I mean, I can have almost any woman I want, and I have. My rep is what it is because I don't date. I fuck. I'm not interested in commitment or settling down. Tried it once before, and all I ended up with was a broken heart and a former best friend.

So no getting attached. No expecting anything more than a good time. I screwed up with Liberty by allowing the lines to blur, and she's still mad at me. Now I'm sure to be clear about the rules with every woman I've been with, and usually avoid anyone I work with. A night, a weekend, once an entire week with a flight attendant on a break—never more than that.

I can't explain what it is with Palmer that makes me want to try again. She's nothing like Angela. Matt can't understand how I can be crazy about a woman I've never been out with, let alone taken to bed. "Once you get in her pants, man, she'll fall right off that pedestal you've got her on," he told me one time when he'd caught me scrolling through her social media feed. "It's the fantasy of the unattainable."

He could be right, but I don't think so. Because when Palmer is around, I'm not thinking about what she'll look like splayed across my bed, what she'll taste like when she cums on my tongue, what sounds she'll make when I hit the right spot. Okay, I'm not *only* thinking of those things. I'm also imagining us cuddling on the couch on a rainy morning or exchanging funny reels throughout the day. Or going out for ice cream, like now.

"So, uh, how are things going? Other than with the game, I mean," I ask, my hands tucked in my pockets so I'm not tempted to touch her and freak her out.

"Been better, I guess," she says with a flat smile. "Found out my boyfriend—*ex* boyfriend—is marrying my cousin."

"Wow."

"Yeah, sums it up." Her chortle is bitter. I want to kick his ass for hurting her.

"Same guy you were living with, I take it?"

"Yeah. Except we broke up in January. New Year's, to be precise."

I raised my brows in surprise. "I didn't know."

"It was the off-season." She shrugs. "I wasn't exactly broadcasting it."

"Huh." She's been single for four months? I had four months to try to woo her and I wasted every one of those days. Stupid. "You okay?"

She shrugs again. "It's fine. I mean, it's not *fine*-fine. It will be fine. What really bothers me is not knowing if Rania was in the picture when we broke up. I feel kind of foolish."

I move in front of her, making her stop. "He's the fool."

"Thanks," she says, skepticism coloring her tone.

"I mean it." I wait for her to look up so I can bend my head to look her straight in the eye. "You're a fucking prize, Palmer, and he's a fool for losing you."

She swallows and blinks her eyes a few times before saying quietly, "Thank you."

I grin. "It's the truth."

I lead her across the street and down another block to Cal's, my favorite soft serve in the neighborhood. The sweet scent of peaches as she squeezes by me puts all my senses on high alert and when she grazes my chest, it's all I can do to command my cock to stand down so I don't embarass myself or her.

"Evenin', Marnie," I greet the middle-aged woman behind the counter holding a large pail.

"Evenin', hon," she replies. "Let me put this one in the back, and I'll be right out."

"So many choices," Palmer says, peering into the cooler.

"Do you prefer it hard or soft?"

She side-eyes me and raises an eyebrow.

I laugh. "Your ice cream, although I think I like where your mind went."

She rolls her eyes, but the corners of her mouth turn up. *Slow your roll, Salinas. Don't scare her away.*

"I like soft serve, but these flavors are calling to me." She taps the window. Marnie returns and offers Palmer a taste. She chooses the black raspberry-chocolate chip combo.

"Mmm," she moans, dragging the flat wooden stick between her lips. I look away as my dick twitches. "So good. Can I try the strawberry-pineapple-fudge swirl?"

Marnie gives her another flat stick. Again, the stick is licked clean and she's making another grunting noise. She's going to fucking kill me if this keeps up.

"I can't decide." Her tongue darts out to lick the corner of her lips while she contemplates the choices. "Can I do a scoop of each in a cup?"

"Of course, hon," Marnie says. She turns to me. "Can I get you something?"

"Soft serve triple twist on a sugar cone, please. And we're together." A touch of color blooms in Palmer's cheeks.

"Thanks, but you don't have to—"

"I want to," I assure her, tapping my card against the reader.

We take our orders and go outside to claim an empty table. It's warm out, but still a school night, so the place isn't too busy. In a few more weeks, we'll be lucky to be in and out in twenty minutes, let alone five. We sit across from one another, which is for the best. I'm still trying to be on my best behavior.

Except I can't help staring as she scoops a spoonful of ice cream and sucks it off the spoon. "So good," she repeats in between tiny whimpers of pleasure. She looks up from her cup and pauses, gesturing at me with her spoon.

"You're dripping."

My mouth dries. "I'm what?"

"Dripping." She points at my cone. "Your ice cream is melting all over your hand."

Sure enough. While I was enraptured by her thorough tasting of the ice cream, my cone melted over the edge of the cone and onto my hand. "Fuck."

I sweep my tongue along the rim of the cone, catching the melting treat before it makes more of a mess. I lick up the sides and suck the top of the cone. Once I tame it into submission with my tongue, I steal a look at Palmer. She's staring back at me, her bright Caribbean eyes darkening to a deep blue.

"Charlie," she starts, setting the cup down. "I have to ask you something, and I need you to let me get it out before you say anything, or I'll lose my nerve."

"Ohh—kay," I say, dragging the word out. Curiosity mixes with concern. "What's up?"

She stares down at her cup of ice cream, then rolls her shoulders back, takes a deep breath, and meets my gaze.

"Seeing Brennan engaged has caused me to question my approach to love. I get too invested, too fast, and what I need—I think—is to try my hand at a no-strings-attached fling. What I'm asking is if you'd do it."

I shake my head, trying to understand if she's asking what I think she's asking. "I'm sorry. Do what?"

"Me, Charlie." She leans across the table, giving me a sweet view of her swells. "I'm asking you to do me."

charlie

THE CONE FALLS from my hand onto the sidewalk and is immediately claimed by a pair of pigeons. But I don't care. Palmer York, the object of my crush for three years, the woman who'd friend-zoned me the moment we met, is asking me to *date* her?

No, not date her. Do her. Sleep with her. *Fuck* her. I'm impossibly hard at the moment, but manage to refrain from picking her up and taking her against the brick wall of the shop. The side of the shop that isn't lit and is mainly covered by bushes.

"I'm sorry, can you—" I wave my hand in the air.

She turns her palms out, like she's holding me back. Probably a good idea. "Let me explain. Because we're friends and I want to be able to stay friends, I need you to understand why I'm asking. I don't want you to think I just want to use you or that I'm a whore—"

"I'd never think that." I'm vehement in my protest, riled she'd ever think I would. "Never."

She smiles. "I appreciate it. But I still need you to know why I'm asking."

She draws in a deep breath. "Brennan and I were together for three years. Things moved pretty fast for us, and we were living together in a matter of months after meeting. I thought we were moving forward.

"But the past year or so, it's been...different. He wasn't happy for me to continue playing. Like my parents, he thought this was a whim. I majored in business with the idea to work for my father's company eventually, but honestly, I love lacrosse. I'm part of something bigger than myself, setting an example for little girls everywhere. Blazing a path for future generations of athletes."

"And you're damn good at it," I interject. She lights up the night with her beaming smile and I promise myself to make her smile like that more often.

"It's my true love." She lifts one shoulder and lets it drop. "Anyway, my family doesn't support me, and Brennan, well, he's like they are. I think he had the impression I'd be discouraged enough to quit if they kept me on the bench. Maybe I would have, except for how great everyone was to me when I first arrived. They've all become another family to me. You know, you were a big reason why I didn't give up."

I raise my eyebrows. "Me?"

Palmer laughs. "Yeah, you. They had a welcome party for all the new members of the team. I was melting into the wall, but you walked over and said, 'Did you know the stadium gets really hot once the game's over? All the fans leave.' You made me laugh, and I was glad I wasn't the only dork in the room."

A laugh bursts out. "Thanks."

She grins. "Then, after I told you my position, you introduced me to Tisha, who has become my mentor and my best friend, and it's all because of you I'm now starting goalie."

I shake my head. "I may have made the introduction, but it is all you, Palmer."

"Anyway," she continues, "I kept playing and our relationship died."

"That's on him," I remind her.

Palmer looked to the side with a frown. "Maybe. But see, it's actually part of a larger problem I have. I tend to get serious with guys super fast. I'm quick to follow my heart and ignore all the red flags in the beginning, which leaves me blindsided and crushed in the end. I want to change that."

She pushed her ice cream to the side and clasped her hands in front of her. "I won't bore you with a rundown of my past, but suffice it to say, my love life has been a series of committed, monogamous relationships. One after another. I've never gone out with a guy for fun. Never had wild, reckless sex. Never picked up a guy in a bar and took him home for a night."

I furrow my brow. "What are you asking, Palmer?"

She chews on her bottom lip and stares at her short, polished nails for a long moment. I stay quiet, giving her room to think and speak. Finally, she lifts her head. Her features are pinched, but the gold in her eyes flashes like a Fourth of July sparkler. She sets her shoulders back and lifts her chin.

"I believe I can break this habit of jumping all in with my heart if I can practice what it's like to take things easy and casual. I need to experience a fling. Sex for the fun of it. Dates without expectations you'll call the next day. A hookup not involving my heart. Everyone knows that's your domain, so I was hoping, as a friend, you could help me out here. Because I really don't want to experiment with a stranger. I trust you."

I release the breath I've been holding, my mind spinning. My dick is more than happy to focus on the fact she wants to have sex with me, and my brain is shouting "Fuck yeah!" But the funny little organ in my chest contracts at the thought of her only wanting my body and not *me*. Yes, I get the irony of that.

"Say something," she pleads. "Anything. Even if it's 'fuck off.' Just. Say. Something."

"Palmer, I consider you a good friend."

Her eyes close and her head drops. All my body parts war with one another to make the right decision. But it's my brain and heart working together that finally cinches it for me. She may only want to use me to experiment with her wild side, but nothing says I can't use this as an opportunity to show her how much more there is to me. Prove I'm not the flippant playboy I let everyone think I am.

"Because you're a good friend, I'll do it."

Her head snaps up, eyes popping wide, lips spread into a blinding smile. "Really?"

I chuckle. "Yeah, really. Did you think I would turn down a proposition like that from a beautiful woman? I may not have gone to an Ivy League like you, but I'm not dumb."

She jumps out of her chair and throws her arms around me. "Thank you, Charlie. You don't know how hard it was to ask you this. I was afraid you'd laugh at me, or worse, run away and avoid me the rest of our lives."

I stand and wrap my arms around her waist. She clasps her hands behind my neck and stares up at me through dark blonde lashes. I touch her forehead with mine. "You never have to worry about telling me or asking me anything. I'm not going to run away."

"One more thing," she says, pulling out of my arms. "Can we keep this between us? I don't want anyone to know we're hooking up. I mean, Tisha knows because I ran this by her. But she's the only one."

My heart drops into my stomach. It's hard not to take the request personally. But I nod and shine a carefree smile at her. "I understand. We work together."

"Right. Exactly." She sighs. "Thanks for understanding."

I pull out my phone and check the rideshare app. "You have a game tomorrow. I have to be up early for work. How about I order you a Lyft?"

Her cute pout is disarming. "You don't want to come back to my place tonight?"

"Not tonight. The first lesson I plan on giving you is how it feels when someone takes his time to worship every inch of your body. We don't have the time tonight, not if we both want to be at the top of our game tomorrow. Where's home?"

"Roland Park." She crinkles her nose as I type in the address. "What about you? Do you want to share?"

I jerk my thumb over my shoulder at the brownstone across the street. "I can walk home."

"I didn't realize you were so close. Will you show me your place sometime?"

"When my brother isn't home." I nod at the lights streaming from the windows. "You can tell he's home because there isn't a light he won't turn on. I think he secretly has stock in BG&E."

We clean up our mess and a few minutes later, a small sedan pulls to the curb. I check the details on the app against the car and, satisfied it's the ride I ordered, open the door for Palmer. She kisses me on the cheek before sliding in and shutting the door. I motion for her to roll down the window.

"You're going to kill it tomorrow."

Her face lights up. "Thank you."

I watch the car drive away until the taillights disappear around the corner before crossing the street. Who knew getting into Palmer York's pants would be the easy part? The challenge is getting into her heart. I'm going to have to convince her I'm more than what everyone saw on the surface and I have no fucking idea how I'm going to do it.

palmer

"CRASH!" I yell at my defenders as the Warriors attack makes a fast break and takes a shot. Defense deflects, but it bounces out of one of their pockets and right back to the offense, who spin and shoot again. I'm ready, dropping my stick to catch the ball as it goes low. The crowd cheers. I count to 9 before leaving the crease, giving my teammates time to get open.

"Clear!" I slide my hand up the shaft and launch the ball toward Ava, our star midfielder and Captain. She catches it on the run, spins around one defender, then makes a quick backward pass to Jewel. The move takes our opponents by surprise, and Jewel handily puts the ball in the net over the goalie's left shoulder.

The whistle blows, ending the game. Baltimore Battle 14, Syracuse Warriors 6. I unsnap my helmet and celebrate the win with my teammates. After shaking hands with our opponents, we head into the locker room for the usual post-game speech by Coach Arkhady.

My heart hitches when I see Charlie at the entrance to the

tunnel filming the team's walk back. He looks up from the viewfinder and catches my eye. His grin stretches across his face, both his dimples on full display. It's contagious, and I return the smile with my own.

"Great game out there," he says as I walk past. "Told you you'd kill it."

I don't get a chance to respond, carried through by a wave of teammates. There is much cheering in the locker room, but once Coach enters, Ava whistles and we all fall silent.

"That was a tremendous start to what is sure to be a stellar season. If we keep up this momentum, if we keep playing hard and making our connections, we can go all the way again this year." She pauses to allow for cheers. "I want to call out our attack line for a superior performance today. We started out a little slow, but by the second period, we were on a roll and we didn't let up.

"Defense," she motions toward the back of the room, where I stand with Andi, Marisol, and Vera, my D-line, "You held the line and kept them to single digits in goal. Excellent job, especially on your part, York. Your first start as goaltender was a massive success. While we all hope for a speedy recovery from Tisha, I think we can be confident we're in good hands with Palmer."

"Hear, hear!" Tisha shouts. I give her a grateful smile.

"Four days until our next game. Go home for tonight, enjoy the win, and get ready to hit it hard at practice tomorrow. Showtime eight a.m. Bring it in."

We move closer together, layering our hands on top of one another. "On 3," Coach directs, "1, 2, 3..."

"Battle! Family!" we all cry, lifting our hands.

After a quick shower, I stand at my locker making sure my equipment is set up for tomorrow. Tisha leans against her locker next to mine. "You going out with the team tonight?"

"I guess." Honestly, I don't want to. I want to find Charlie. I'm anxious for my first lesson. Last night, it took me a while after I got home to unwind and settle into bed. When I finally found sleep, he invaded my dreams, and I woke up wet, restless, and needy. It probably says something that in three years with Brennan, I never woke up like that.

"You have to come celebrate," she says. "We're only going to Harbor Lights. Nothing too crazy. It's Karaoke Night."

I roll my eyes. "Okay, but I'm not singing."

Tisha pouts, sticking her lip out for maximum effect. "Who's going to be Sporty Spice when we do 'Wannabe'?"

"Ask one of the rookies," I suggest. "It'll make them feel like part of the team."

Tisha clicks her tongue. "You're no fun."

"Yeah, I know. I'm trying to fix that," I say with a grin.

"Oh yeah?" Tisha waggles her eyebrows. "Anyone helping?"

"Maybe," I say, concentrating hard on my gym bag. There hadn't been time before the game today to tell her about last night.

"Is it Charlie? Please say it's Charlie."

I sigh and Tisha squeals. I motion with my hand to keep it down. "We had a nice time last night, and I, um, propositioned him. I asked him to help me experiment with being more casual."

"I take it he said yes?" Tisha claps her hands together. "Ooh, I knew it. You played better because you let that man give you an orgasm."

"Actually, no," I correct her. "He said he'd help, but then he put me in a car and sent me home." I tell Tisha what Charlie had said about taking his time.

Tisha fans herself. "Girl, I know the man has game. But that's a whole other level. I'd better get details."

"When I have them."

We walk out together and join the other players heading out for dinner. I attempt to be casual while I look for Charlie among the crowd, disappointed when I don't see him. But now is the time to bond with my team, and for once, I could go out and not worry about Brennan waiting for me at home or the fight we'd inevitably have if I were out too late.

"Palmer."

Charlie comes up behind me. He nods at Tisha and smiles. "Hey, Tisha."

"Hi, Charlie," she says in a singsong voice. I side-eye her, but she ignores me. "We're going out for Karaoke and dinner at Harbor Lights. Wanna join?"

He scratches the back of his neck. "Thanks, but this is a moment for your team. Although, let me know the next time. I'd love to video Marisol doing Karaoke. She has some pipes."

"She'd love that." Tisha winks at Palmer. "I'll meet you at the car."

"So, what's up?" I ask Charlie, ignoring the nervous twist in my stomach.

"I wanted to congratulate you." One side of his mouth quirks up. "And ask if you were free tomorrow night for dinner?"

"Yes. Of course." I glance around and lower my voice. "My first lesson?"

His mouth tightens a fraction, but then he grins. "Sure, if you'd like. But I want to take you out to dinner. Whatever happens after," he shrugs, "we'll let it happen organically. Sound good?"

"Yeah, sounds great." I'm not entirely sure what he means

about letting things happen organically. He's a player, which is why I'm doing this.

"Okay then. Well, have a good time tonight." He tugs a lock of my hair, then disappears down the hall. Clearing my thoughts, I walk out. Tonight is about my team. Tomorrow is about starting my education—my *awakening*—with Charlie, and I can't wait.

charlie

"WHY ARE YOU SO HAPPY?" my brother grumbles when I stride into the kitchen whistling. His black hair standing up on one side, he shovels a spoonful of Captain Crunch into his mouth and mumbles something.

"Chew, swallow, talk, dude," I scold, pouring myself a glass of orange juice. "Come on, we learned that in Kindergarten."

Matt finishes his bite of cereal and tries again. "I asked if you got laid last night."

"Nope." I let my lips pop on that syllable.

"Then why the whistling?" Matt acts offended by my cheerful disposition, so I dial it up. I blast him with my sunniest smile.

"I'm happy. The Battle won their first game yesterday." I take a drink of juice and scroll through my phone, acting nonchalant.

"Yeah, I saw the post on Insta." Matt takes another bite of cereal and slits his eyes at me while he chews. "Also saw your girl had a hell of a start."

My lips split into another smile, this one involuntary and genuine. Matt notices. He smirks, pointing at me with his spoon. "You're so whipped and she's not even your girlfriend."

"I'm whipped?" I bark out a laugh. "Rich coming from the man who canceled his annual boys' trip to Vegas so he could take his girlfriend to see N'Sync."

"It was BTS, and when you're in a relationship with someone, you make compromises. You're not in a relationship with this girl."

"Not yet," I say, not looking up from my phone.

"I thought she already had a boyfriend."

"*Had* being the operative word." I glance up at him. "They broke up."

Matt stabs at the cereal. "Nice. Rebounds are the best. No one has any expectations. Maybe you can finally get her out of your system and not have to worry about her getting too attached."

I sigh and take a seat at the table, putting my phone down. "What if I want her to get attached?"

My brother chews slowly and swallows. "Do you?"

I nod. "Yeah. Yeah, I think I do."

The spoon clatters in his bowl. Matt sits back and folds his arms. "Shit. After Angela, I thought you wrote all women off."

Hearing my ex's name is a cold, soggy sponge to my head, but I shake it off and picture Palmer's eyes. "I thought I did, too. I told you, man, there's something about Palmer I can't explain. She lights me up."

"Dude," Matt laughs. He picks up his bowl and carries it to the sink. "You're pussy whipped already and you haven't even gotten into–"

"Don't. Fucking. Say. It," I growl, clenching my fist.

"All right, no need to punch me. Again." He rubs the bridge of his nose. "So you gonna ask her out or what?"

"We're going out tonight."

"Thought you didn't want to be a rebound?"

Is that what I am? No, not really. A sliver of doubt creeps in, but I brush it aside. "It's not like that. All right, look–I shouldn't tell you this, so swear you won't open your big mouth."

"Who am I gonna tell?" Matt rolls his eyes at my glare. "Fine. I swear."

"I'm not looking to be her rebound, but we do have sort of a thing. Her ex is a total piece of shit and he's completely wrecked her confidence." I tell him what happened with the douche and Palmer's cousin, and how it's made her rethink her whole dating philosophy. "So now, she thinks she needs to learn how to have a casual fling so she won't keep falling in love with douchebags. She knows I—*date*—around, we're friends, she trusts me, so she asked me to help her out."

"Wait, wait," Matt closes his eyes and holds up a finger. "Let me get this straight. She wants you to teach her sex tricks?"

I grimace. "More that she wants to see what it's like to screw around, have a bit of casual fun outside of a serious relationship. Do something a little crazy."

"But you just said you want an attachment."

"Yeah, I know." I run a hand through my hair, pushing it back off my forehead. "A minor obstacle."

Matt chuckles. "She wants to get her freak on, then move on. You want the total opposite. How is that minor?"

"She thinks I'm a big player–"

"You are."

"Ok, yeah, I am. But I'm going to show here there's more to me. I'm going to show her how she deserves to be treated and that I'm the man who will treat her that way." I blow out a breath. "I've got the season to convince her. You were as bad as me until you met Bianca. You managed to win her over."

"Yeah, but I'm me and you're you."

I flip him the bird and he laughs. "Seriously, bro. How do you plan to do it?"

"Romance her, for starters," I say. "Make her feel like the goddess she is. Cheer her on, listen to her. Make her feel so good she won't be able to imagine ever sleeping with anyone else again."

"What if it doesn't work?" Matt shrugs. "What if you do all those things and then at the end of the season, she says, 'It's been fun. Thanks for the memories'?"

The sliver of doubt returns. I try to swallow it, but it cuts on its way down. "Not gonna happen."

"But what if it does?" Matt presses. "Come on, *Carlito*. As your older brother and the one who had a front-row seat to the Angela disaster, the last thing I want is for you spiral out again. You remember how it was."

Matt was the one who was there to pick up my pieces in the aftermath of walking in on Angela and Peter. In one horrifying minute, just months before graduating from college, I lost the girl I was ready to marry and my best friend since childhood. It was Matt who drove down to the Eastern Shore to take me home. Helped me find a place to live while I finished off the term and made sure I graduated. For the past decade, I've done my best to avoid running into either of them. No small feat considering Pete's folks still lived next door to mine. It was one of the reasons I jumped at the chance to move from the offices at the Annapolis stadium to Baltimore.

I flex my jaw. "There's no chance of Palmer fucking my best friend, since I don't have one anymore. She's not like that, anyway.

"Besides," I continue. "Weren't you the one telling me I shouldn't let what happened define the rest of my life? That I shouldn't give up on someday finding the right woman? Well... I think I have."

Matt sighs. "I don't want you hurt again."

"I know. I appreciate it. But trust me, I know what I'm doing."

"I hope so, man. I sure hope so."

I'm too busy at work to look for Palmer. I spend most of the day in the office, cutting B-roll and creating evergreen content for our social media. I can't stop my thoughts from oscillating between Palmer and what my brother said. She's a beast in the goal, but Palmer is the sweetest person off the field. She's also been betrayed by someone who was supposed to love her. I can't imagine she could or would do that to another person.

I'm focused on my screen and startle when Liberty suddenly perches herself on my desk.

She laughs. "Am I that scary?"

You can be. I give her a tight smile. "Surprised me is all."

She crosses her legs, the hem of the suede skirt she wears riding up to reveal a smooth, pale thigh. I swivel in my chair and slide back a few inches to make sure there's no accidental touching.

I lean back. "What can I do for you, Liberty?"

She smoothes the sides of her sleek auburn coiff. "What's going on between you and Palmer York?"

I fold my hands and rest them against my stomach. "What do you mean?"

She scoffs. "Oh, come on. The other night, you could barely keep your tongue in your mouth. And since when are players ever invited to our happy hours?"

"Since I happened to see her. Why shouldn't we invite

players or any of our other colleagues to our post-work happy hours?" I ignore her comment about my tongue because it's probably true. But it's none of her business.

"It just seems like an odd choice," Liberty says drily, inspecting her dark crimson talons.

"What's an odd choice? Inviting a friend to hang out?"

"Deny all you want. You were trying to get her into bed, if you haven't already." She cocks her head and lower her voice. "I'm just saying. You're a big guy, but Palmer is a big girl. I can't imagine you can do the things to her that you used to do to me. Pick me up and take me against the wall. That thing we did in the shower–"

"Enough," I snap. I straighten in my chair and brush the hair off my face. "Look, Liberty. I have apologized for hurting your feelings. I have done everything I can to try to make it up to you. You can hate me all you want; I can't stop you. You can forgive me, and we can move on. Or you don't, and *I* move on. Either way, I'm not playing this game with you anymore. If you'll excuse me, I have to finish this."

I gesture at the screens she's partially blocking. She draws in a breath and hops off the desk. I scoot back into place and put my hands on the mouse, ready to continue. But Liberty still stands there.

"I don't hate you," she says quietly. "I wish I did."

She walks away before I can respond, stiff spined but graceful, and for the hundredth time I castigate myself for being a complete dick. I scrub a hand over my face and go back to work.

NINE

palmer

RIDING HIGH on our first win of the season, practice went off without a hitch. We ran drills all morning, hitting all the fundamentals of scooping, cradling, and passing. I practiced clearing with Donovan, the goalie coach, and Jackie, with Tisha encouraging us and offering tips. After a shower and lunch, we watched game film in the meeting room and broke down the Stars' offensive and defensive plays. Our new offensive coordinator, Coach Kayla, did an impressive job of pointing out the subtle flaws in the Philadelphia team's defense. Afterward, I approach her to tell her so.

"Thanks," she says. "I know it's nerdy to say this, but I honestly love poring over game film and finding all the nuances, so we can exploit them and kick their asses."

I laugh. "You're from Ohio?"

"Mm-hm."

"Did you play at Ohio State?"

She hesitates, then flashes a quick grin. "I went to a small liberal arts school outside Columbus. It was barely DIII. I played for a couple of years, but had to give it up."

I couldn't imagine giving up my career. Even in the face of

my parents' disapproval, I've stuck with it. It's my one form of rebellion. "Well, you're a great coach. Too bad you couldn't keep playing."

She swipes through her phone and turns it around so I can see the photo on her screen. It's a little girl, maybe seven or eight, smiling wide enough to show her two missing front teeth. "Some things mean more than the game."

"She's adorable. What's her name?"

"Shea." She looks at the photo once more before switching off the screen and putting it back in her pocket. "You know, you're looking good out there, too. Keep up the good work."

She pats me on the shoulder and says her goodbyes to the room. I check my watch. It's three-thirty. I shoot a text to Charlie as I head out of the building.

ME

> We're released. What time did you want to meet up?

His reply comes a few seconds later.

CHARLIE

I'm off at five. Pick you up around six?

ME

> I can meet you somewhere. Save you the crosstown trip.

CHARLIE

Absolutely not. A gentleman picks up his date.

ME

> I thought you didn't date.

CHARLIE

I'm still a gentleman. 🎩 Text me your address.

ME

What should I wear?

CHARLIE

Whatever you're most comfortable in.

ME

My pajamas?

CHARLIE

Depends. Are we talking sleepshirt or shirt
and pants?

ME

Tank top and tiny shorts.

CHARLIE

You're killing me, Smalls. 💀 I'm trying to be
gentlemanly.

ME

What if I don't want you to be a gentleman?
😈

CHARLIE

That'll come later... and so will you. When it's
time. 😈

I make it home in record time to get ready.

I've just finished adjusting my breasts and second-guessing my
choice of attire when the intercom buzzes. Six sharp. Charlie is
hot *and* punctual.

I check the camera to confirm it's him and press the button
to let him up. A minute later, there's a knock on the door. I take
a deep breath, then open it. "Right on time."

His smile freezes in place. His eyes wander down my body,
then back up, pausing on my breasts before moving to my

mouth and finally my eyes. His Adam's Apple bobs with a swallow. "Wow."

My neck heats, the flush creeping its way up to my cheeks. "Not too much?"

He traces the sweetheart neckline, tickling the skin of my bosom, and shakes his head. "Are you comfortable?"

"Yes, and... it has pockets." I put my hands in the pockets of the coral sundress I chose and twirl, the scalloped hem emblazoned with hummingbirds flaring out so it looked like the birds were in flight. It's one of the few pieces of my wardrobe chosen by my mother I actually liked.

Charlie whistles. "Very nice. But we should go now, or we may not make it out of here."

He offers his elbow and I slip my hand through. I grab my keys and crossbody with my other hand and shut the door, checking the auto-lock engaged. "So where are we going?"

"You'll see."

He guides me out the door to his car, which is double-parked. "I should've given you the garage code so you could park underneath," I say, sliding into the front seat of the dark blue Toyota.

"Next time." He closes the door and walks around to the driver's side. Traffic in Baltimore on a Friday evening is its typical clusterfuck, but at last we're on the beltway heading out of town.

I scroll through the saved stations on his satellite radio to distract myself from my nerves and select a surprising one. Dolly Parton sings about love being like a butterfly. "I wouldn't have pegged you as a country fan."

He laughs. "Classic country. I grew up listening to Dolly, Patsy, Merle, Kenny."

"Johnny Cash?"

He scoffs and gives me an incredulous look. "Of course."

"Huh." I settle back in my seat. "We've been friends for a few years now, but I know shockingly little about you. So tell me. Who is Charlie Salinas?"

The corner of his lips pulls up, showing a hint of a dimple. "Just a guy taking a beautiful woman out on this lovely May night."

"Seriously." I face him best I can with the seatbelt restraining me. "You know all about me since you did the interview. But where are you from? You said you have a brother—is he your only sibling? What's your sign? How old are you, for that matter? Is Charlie short for Charles, or is it just Charlie?"

He shoots a glance my way. "All right. I'm from Annapolis. I have one brother, Matt. I'm a Cancer, I think. I'm thirty-three. And neither."

"Neither? What do you mean, neither? What else is Charlie short for?"

"Carlos," he says with a laugh. "My name is Carlos Alejandro Salinas. My brother Matt is Mateo. My grandparents immigrated from Mexico fifty years ago, when my father was ten, and he faced a lot of racism growing up as Miguel. He didn't want that for us, but he still wanted to honor our roots. My grandparents and extended family call us Carlos and Mateo, but to the rest of the world, we're Charlie and Matt. Although my brother's girlfriend calls him Matty, but she's the only one allowed to."

"Noted." I chuckle, then frown. "How do you feel about that? Does it ever seem like you're hiding who you are?"

He purses his lips. "I guess I never thought about it. I don't hide that I'm Mexican-American, but it doesn't come up all that often."

"Do you speak Spanish? I tried to learn French, but it didn't go well. We took a trip to Paris and I tried to practice, but everyone I spoke to pleaded with me to stop assaulting their language and *parlee-voos-Anglish*." I snicker when I catch him wincing. "It's okay, you can laugh. I know it's terrible."

He laughs with me. "I can get by, but I'm most fluent in swear words. I was a brat as a kid and I didn't want to learn. Matt's a natural. He can hold conversations with my parents and often does, just to tick me off."

"What do your mom and dad do?"

"Mom was a seamstress," he says, pride evident in his voice. "Had her own shop doing custom tailoring until the arthritis. My dad was a carpenter. He retired after forty years with the same company and now takes on the odd custom woodworking gig so he and my mom can travel."

"So that's where your creativity comes from. I'm impressed."

He snorted. "Hardly. I've never been very good at handiwork like my parents and my brother. He's a professional carpenter like our dad."

"Don't sell yourself short." I squeeze his arm. My hand lingers on the hard muscle underneath, and when he flexes, I remove my hand and try to hide my blush.

Charlie's dimples deepen, but he doesn't mention it. He exits the highway, but I've missed the sign announcing where we're going. "What about your parents?" he asks. "Do they go to many games? I could make sure we get some footage at the next one, if they'd be okay with it."

I twist the fabric of my skirt as I answer. "They haven't seen me play since college. I think I told you before, they don't consider this a real job. I'm supposed to go to work for my dad until I find a suitable husband, pop out a few grandchildren, and join my mother on her charity boards. It's embarrassing to them that I play a sport, while their friends' kids are all CEOs or lawyers or doctors, or married to CEOs, lawyers, or doctors.

The only time I've ever done something they actually approved of was moving in with Brennan."

Charlie does a doubletake, which would have been comical if it weren't in response to my pathetic reality. "You're kidding, right?"

"No. They loved Brennan. He was clean-cut, worked for a prestigious finance firm, wore Brooks Brothers and Ferragamo. Golfed with my dad, helped connect mom with donors. At least with him marrying my cousin, they'll keep him in the family."

Charlie is silent for a long moment, so long I regret letting all that spill out. He's taking me out because I asked him to teach me how to have casual sex, essentially. He already knows I'm pathetic. I don't need to hammer the point home.

"You're amazing. I'm sorry your parents can't see that."

He puts his hand on my knee and squeezes. I give him a surprised smile, covering his hand with my own. I'm saved from having to respond when he turns down a dirt road leading to an oversized barn. He pulls into a marked spot and turns off the engine.

"We're here."

TEN

charlie

I HELP Palmer out of the car and lead her around the side of the barn. An older woman with a long silver braid greets us. "Hi, Charlie."

"Miss Annabelle." I kiss her cheek. I step back and put my hand on Palmer's back. "This is Palmer. Palmer, this is Miss Annabelle."

Palmer shakes Miss Annabelle's hand. "Lovely to meet you."

"I've heard so much about you," Miss Annabelle says. "It's nice to meet you finally."

"You have?" Palmer turns quizzical eyes my way.

I glance away and rub the back of my neck. "I might have mentioned you once or twice. Along with other people from work."

Palmer suppresses a grin as Miss Annabelle leads us into the barn. Though barn isn't an accurate description. Annabelle and her husband have converted the building into an elegant country restaurant. A dozen tables covered in pristine white cloths dot the space. Overhead, white string lights crisscross through the beams, while bronze sconces bathe the area in a warm glow. Along one side stretches a polished oak bar, stocked with top-tier alcohol lined up along mirrored shelves. In the back, a cutout in the wall gives a glimpse of the stainless steel kitchen behind it.

"This is beautiful," Palmer says, looking around. "The bar is gorgeous."

"Thank you." Miss Annabelle gestures toward me. "Well, thank Charlie's brother, Matt. He custom-built the bar."

"So when's the big opening?" I ask, admiring the scrollwork on the molding. Matt really is good. Not that I'd tell him—his ego is big enough.

"Next week." Miss Annabelle leads us to the only table set with crystal, china, and silverware and motions for us to sit down. I pull out the chair for Palmer, then take the one next to her.

"Wait," Palmer says, turning in her seat. "Is this *The* Barn? I heard a story about your opening. Chef Nate Faulkner helped design your menu."

"That's right," Miss Annabelle says, pride shining from her eyes. "We were lucky to get his help."

"Miss Annabelle is gracious enough to let us be a test case before they open," I explain.

"We aren't fully stocked yet and the bartender doesn't begin until next week, so aside from sparkling or still water, I can offer you a Pinot Grigio or Cabernet from a local vineyard."

Palmer orders a Pinot. Miss Annabelle turns to me. "Charlie?"

"I'll have the same, thanks."

After Miss Annabelle leaves to get our drinks, Palmer leans her elbows on the table, her eyes wide and her amazing tits on full display. "I can't believe I'm going to be one of the first people to eat at The Barn. My parents will die. I know they made reservations but couldn't get an opening for a couple of months."

I drag my gaze away from her chest and to her eyes, but that doesn't do much to help my scrambling brain. Looking into her eyes is like looking into a tropical sea, the light gold ring around the iris an island I could happily live on for the rest of my life. *Damn.* Matt is right. I am whipped.

"Charlie?" Palmer giggles. "Are you listening to me?"

I blink and dip my head, giving her a sheepish grin. "I was momentarily distracted. You have the most beautiful eyes."

Her lips part. A lovely pink blush blooms in her cheeks. She dips her head as she tucks her hair behind her ears. "They're weird. But thank you."

"What?" I'm stunned. "They're not weird, they're gorgeous. Unique. Who would ever tell you otherwise?"

She glances at me, then darts her eyes away. Anger sparks and simmers in my stomach. "It was the prick you were dating."

Palmer takes in a sharp breath, then forces a smile. "Actually, no. But I don't want to talk about them or him. Or even think about any of it." She takes my hand.

I squeeze. "Listen. There is nothing weird about you. Your eyes, your smile, your body–Palmer, you're a walking wet dream."

Her lips part again, her eyes darkening while a delicious flush colors her chest. This is aroused Palmer, and I like her a hell of a lot more than embarrassed Palmer.

I'm seconds from suggesting we blow off dinner so I can take her somewhere to show her exactly how sexy she is when Miss Annabelle returns with our drinks. "It's a fixed menu tonight," she says. "Based on what we have available on the farm. We have braised sausage and fennel, or, if you prefer meatless, we have wild mushroom mezzalune in a creamy garlic alfredo. Both served with homemade sourdough and a fresh garden salad. All main ingredients sourced from right here on the farm."

"They both sound so good," Palmer says, her eyes lighting up.

"We'll have one of each," I say. "Then we can share."

"Perfect." Miss Annabelle claps her hands together. "It'll be out shortly."

After what can only be described as the best meal I've ever eaten, with the best dinner date I've ever had, we say our good-byes to Miss Annabelle with compliments to the chef and leave.

"This has been great, Charlie," Palmer says. She reaches her hand over the console and I take it, interlacing our fingers.

"It's not over yet," I inform her with a wink.

"Are we going back to my place?" she asks, the hopeful excitement in her voice almost making me forget my plans.

"One more stop. Trust me, you'll love it." I wink at her.

I pull into the parking lot of a strip mall and help her out of the car. "What is this place?" she asks, looking up at the sign above the door of the first storefront. "ShatterZone?"

"You'll see." I hold open the door and follow behind her. The girl at the desk inside greets us with a smile. "Welcome to ShatterZone. Do you have a reservation?"

"Yes, for Salinas."

The girl checks on the computer, then hands over two passes. "You are in room three. Down the hall and on your right. Lisa will help you put on the safety suits."

"Great. Thanks." I take Palmer's free hand and lead her down the hall.

"Uh, safety suit?" Palmer raises a brow at me. I chortle.

"Just wait."

I open the door to room three and we step inside a small vestibule. Another young woman is inside unfolding a white Tyvek suit. She looks up and smiles at us.

"Hi. You must be Palmer and Charlie. Do you have your passes?"

I hand over the cards, and after taking a cursory glance at them, she gives each of us one of the suits. We climb into them and zip them up. Lisa helps us put up our hoods and slide a plastic face shield over our heads. Then she puts thick rubber gloves on each of us and has Palmer don a pair of rubber boots over her sandals. "No open-toe shoes," she chirps.

Palmer gives me one more questioning look before Lisa opens another door at the back of the vestibule. She ushers us inside.

"Feel free to use whatever tool you'd like. We have bats, clubs, pipes—your choice. When the light turns red," she points to a fixture above the door currently blinking green, "your time is up. As soon as the light turns solid green, you can start. Have a smashing time!" She waves and then slips out the door.

Palmer turns in a circle and takes in the room full of glass. Crystal vases, porcelain dishes, mirrors, and shelves full of other glass artifacts are waiting to be smashed to smithereens. "You brought me to a rage room?"

The light turns solid green. I pick up a bat and nod at her to choose her weapon. "I thought you might have some residual rage you wanted to get rid of."

Palmer's face glows and even behind the warped plastic shield, I can see her huge smile. "I love it."

She hefts one of the lightweight pipes and raises it above her head. She cracks her neck from side to side. "Let's do this."

ELEVEN

WHEN WE RETURN to my place, I direct Charlie to the garage entrance. He parks and we ride the elevator to my floor. We don't speak; the air thrums with anticipation. His thumb moves in small circles on the back of my hand as he holds it, each pass over my skin sending a current straight to my clit. When the doors open, I practically drag him down the hall to my door. My hands tremble when I try to put the key in the lock, which becomes even more difficult when he pushes behind me, his hot breath skating across the back of my neck. He grasps my hip with one hand and moves my hair to the side with the other, exposing a spot behind my ear I didn't know was so sensitive until he presses a light kiss to it.

"Need help getting it in?" he murmurs. His low, velvety timbre zings right to my core and I nearly drop the keys.

I breathe out a nervous laugh. "Isn't that why you're here? To help me?"

By some miracle I unlock the door and together we tumble inside. The door shuts behind us, and he spins me toward him, cupping my face in his hands and holding me still as his mouth crashes down on mine. He licks into my seam, and once I'm past the initial surprise of his touch, I meet his tongue stroke for stroke. My hands roam up his back, reveling in the heat of his skin and hard, muscular contours through his shirt. I scratch my nails across his traps then let my hands drift to the tight curve of his ass.

He groans and walks me backward until my back hits the wall beside the couch. I try to guide him to my right, to the more comfortable cushions, but he growls–*growls*–and the sound not only stops me, but makes my already damp panties wetter. I whimper when he presses his hardness against the juncture of my thighs, all the while continuing to plunder my needy mouth. I part my legs and move my hips, hands delving in the waistline of his pants to clench his perfect ass and push him harder into me, seeking the precious friction of his clothing-covered cock against my clit.

He kisses his way down from my lips to my chin to the side of my neck and suckles on the sensitive skin at the curve of my neck and shoulder. I tilt my head for more access, moaning as his hands squeeze my breasts, lifting them to meet his lips as he spreads kisses across the top of them.

I love the feel of his mouth on me, but bending causes him to move and I lose the sweet pressure on my most sensitive nerves. I hiss in frustration and pull him back agains me. He laughs against my skin.

"Needy little girl, aren't you?" he rasps.

I bite my lip and look up at him. "Are you going to give me what I need? Is this my first lesson?"

His smile tightens for a moment, but then his dimples appear and his eyes glint in the soft light from the floor lamp I'd left on. "Sure. If you want to call it that."

"What would you call it?" I ask breathlessly as his hands slide up the hem of my dress to my very lacy, very wet bikini briefs.

"Dessert." He licks his lips. "I didn't have any at The Barn, and I like to end my evenings on something sweet."

My eyes, half-lidded as a haze of lust clouds my brain, fly open. He kisses me, this time slow and probing, his tongue moving in and out from between my lips in a steady rhythm. His fingers twist in the side of my panties as he starts pushing them down.

"I bet you're sweet, baby. I bet you'll taste like peaches and berries," he murmurs against my lips. His fingers slick through my wetness and his moan joins mine. "You're wet. So fucking wet. Is this all for me?"

My nod is jerky as anxiety wars with the desperate, greedy need inside me. No one, especially not Brennan, has ever expressed any interest in tasting me. On rare occasions, he'd return the favor, but he didn't enjoy it, which meant I didn't enjoy it. What if there's something about me–

"Where did you go?" Charlie whispers, bringing me back to the present. His hand stops moving, and he draws it out from under my dress.

"I–nowhere–I," I stammer. I close my eyes, my cheeks on fire. I'm ruining the moment. "Let's keep going."

"Hey. Hey," Charlie holds my hip with one hand and lightly caresses my cheek with the other. "You gotta be in this with me, babe. You've got to tell me if I'm doing something you don't like."

"What if it's something you might not like?" I lower my gaze.

"Honey, I can't think of a single thing I wouldn't like to do with, or to, you." He lifts my chin. "What do you think I won't like? Because so far, I'm in fucking heaven."

I swallow, ashamed to say it out loud and mad at myself for dumping a bucket of cold, or at least lukewarm, water on us.

I'm saved from having to speak the words when his expression clears and I see the lightbulb turn on.

His lids lower. "Do you think I won't like eating you?" I lift a shoulder. He nuzzles his forehead against mine. "Honey, I'm gonna say this once and only once. Forget anything that bastard ever told you or made you feel. This is about you and me. No one else, okay? I need you here with me and only me."

I reply with a hard, hungry kiss, a promise to do precisely that. When his fingers once again push through my tight curls, thoughts of anyone who came before this moment evaporate like dew on a sunwashed field. I gasp when his finger pushes inside, pulsing in and out, drawing even more wetness from my body. I've never been so turned on. I squirm under his touch, and when he adds a second finger, then begins circling his thumb around my nub. I pant as the need for release builds inside me.

"Do you like this?" he asks in between punishing kisses.

"Yes," I gasp. It's the only word I am capable of forming as the pressure continues to build and build. "Yes. Yes. Yesss."

His fingers move faster. I pump my hips to meet his thrusts. "That's it, baby," he whispers in my ear, showering kisses down my neck. "Fuck my hand. That's a good girl. You're so tight around my fingers. Imagine how good my cock is going to feel when I finally slide home."

I mewl and writhe, the end so close, on the cusp of release. I don't know what to do with my hands—I want to touch him everywhere all at once the way. While he fucks me with his right hand, he takes my wrist in his left one and moves it to my chest.

"Pull your tit our for me, baby," he growls, sucking hard on the swell of my breast. I tug the neckline down and reach in to release my breast from the demi-cup I'm wearing. It spills out the top, a thrill racing through my body as Charlie's eyes turn even darker. "Hold it for me."

I lift my heavy mound to his lips. With one hand braced on the wall next to my head and the other curling inside my slick heat while he flicked my clit with his thumb, he took my stiff peak between his lips and sucked, scraping his teeth along the nipple then soothing with his hot tongue.

The sensations coursing through me are too much. I cry out his name, my hips bucking against his hand as he fucks me harder with his fingers, pulling and tugging on my nipple until I can't take it anymore. The dam inside me breaks, my release spilling over and out of me as I convulse in his arms. He lets go of my breast and pulls my head into his shoulder, pulling his fingers slowly out of my pussy as the last of the aftershocks shudder through my body leaving me breathless and limp in his arms.

"Fuck, Charlie," I choke, resting my head on his shoulder. "That was... fuck..."

"My sentiments exactly. Hey, look at me." I drag my heavy-lidded gaze to his face. He holds up two glistening fingers, the ones I'd just fucked like I was on fire, and draws his lips over one licking it clean. His eyes close briefly, and he moans. "So sweet."

He holds the other finger to my lips. "See how good you taste."

When I clamp my lips around his finger and sample my own tangy cream, I'm rewarded with a wolfish grunt from Charlie, his eyes so dark and feral it stokes my arousal again. When he bends to his knees, I am ready–eager, even–for him to do to me with his mouth what he just did with his fingers.

But instead, he simply pulls my panties back up, smoothing them into place, then tucks my loose breast back into my dress and straightens our clothes. At my confused look, he gives me a sly, one-dimpled grin. "I should get home. And you need rest. Tomorrow's your last practice before your away game in Iowa."

I crinkle my brow. "But you didn't, you know—," I wave my hand, "finish."

He kisses my forehead and steps back, a slight wince the only indication of his discomfort. "Lesson one: A real man will make sure you're taken care of with no expectations on his part. Besides, I need to leave you a reason to want me to come back."

"You'll be back, then?" I bite my lip, knowing the answer but anxious nonetheless.

He brushes a light kiss against my lips, following it with a swift smack on my ass. "Just try to keep me away."

palmer

"PALMER, GIRL, YOU ARE ON FIRE!"

Tisha wraps her arms around me and nearly squeezes the life out of me. "Oof, Tish. I need at least one lung to keep playing."

"A shutout!" she shouts. "It's been two years since my last shutout."

"It's the defense," I demur, stripping off my jersey and unsnapping my pads. I hang them on the hook in my locker and toss my jersey in the hamper by the lockers. The equipment managers will sanitize and pack everything up before they leave tonight. "They did a great job keeping them out of the arc and avoiding shooting space calls. I only had a handful of shots I needed to block."

"Yeah, our defense rocks," Tisha concedes. "But you did more than block a few shots. You called out the field to them, you put them in the right place to make a strong defense. You led out there on the field like you should and that's what got us the win."

"That and Jewel's fast breaks," Andi, one of the defenders,

speaks up. "She was a rocket after face-off. You'd think by the second quarter they'd have figured it out."

"They did," I say. "Their defense stepped it up and held us to single digits for the rest of the game. But they're not as good as our defense."

I fist bump Andi. The excited chatter in the locker room grows quiet when Coach Arkhady walks in to give her post-game speech. As she begins, Tisha leans over and whispers in my ear, "Orgasms helping your game, huh?"

I side-eye her and she laughs quietly. "Don't make me regret telling you," I grumble.

After Coach's speech and a refreshing shower, I gather my things and follow my teammates out to the bus that will take us back to the hotel. Our flight home was early in the morning. Tisha walks out with me, trying to hide her wince. I nod at her knee brace. "Bothering you again?"

"You mean 'still'?" She sighs. "Don't tell anyone, but the last time I met with the docs and we went over the latest imaging, the prognosis is replacement surgery in my future. I've done more than tear a ligament, apparently. Doesn't look like I'll see the field at all this season."

"Damn, Tisha. I'm so sorry."

She shrugs, then pulls me away from the crowd while we wait for the rest of the team to come out. "It's a good thing I was planning an early retirement, or I'd be more upset. But the team is in good hands with you in the crease and, frankly, I'm ready. I've had a stick in my hand since I was four. I love it. But Manny and I have been thinking about moving. A great opportunity for him came up, but it means relocating to Wyoming."

Manny and Tisha married a few years ago. He's a defense contractor in the communications field working out of Fort

Meade. My mouth drops. "So you're not only leaving the team, you're leaving the area?"

Tisha hoists her bag further up on her shoulder. "Looks like it. We've been thinking about having a family. But let's face it. Maryland is freakin' expensive. With a bump in pay and a lower cost of living, we could own a house, two cars, and if I wanted to stay home with a baby I could."

"Your mother won't like it," I tease.

"I've dropped hints, but she's ignoring them. I may need to find a place that will allow us to move her in with us."

I giggle. "Bet Manny would love it."

Tisha rolls her eyes. "I swear, he should be her child and I should be the in-law. She's probably more upset about him moving than her only daughter."

"Don't say anything to the rest of the team, though," Tisha reminds me, unnecessarily. Of course, I won't share her news. "Hey, maybe we can double with you and Charlie this weekend. After our Saturday home game, we don't play again until Thursday, so Coach will give us the weekend off. Want to do something Saturday night?"

"I don't think that'd be a good idea," I said with a grimace. "This thing with Charlie and me isn't supposed to involve double dating. That's what couples do and we are not a couple."

"You don't have to be committed to join your friends for dinner. Charlie's my friend, too. It doesn't have to be weird. I promise not to bring up how he took you glass-smashing, then you did some smashing against the wall."

My insides heat as they do whenever I replay that night in my mind. It was only a few days ago, but it feels like both eons and only hours. I haven't seen Charlie since we left for the game. He didn't travel with us this time. I miss him, but I'm not supposed to. You missed your boyfriend, not your hookup.

I'm determined to remind myself he is firmly in the latter category, not the former. I shake my head. "It's too intimate."

"All right, I get it," Tisha's look tells me she doesn't really. But she doesn't press. "If you change your mind, let me know."

My phone vibrates as I find a seat on the bus, and I can't help the way my heart kicks thinking it's Charlie. He'd texted me before the game to wish me luck, a text I ignored only for the fact I wanted to reply so desperately. I shouldn't be so eager to reply to someone I'm only sleeping with. But I'll reply to him now, because whatever else, he is still my friend. It makes sense in my head.

Unfortunately, it isn't Charlie. It's my father. He hates talking on the phone, while my mother hates texting. Sometimes, if they were both mad at me for something—a common occurrence—I would get calls from Mom followed by a barrage of texts from Dad. I've been avoiding my mother, so I'm not surprised to hear from him.

> **DAD**
> Come for dinner tonight. We need to talk to you and your mother hasn't been able to reach you.

> **ME**
> Can't. I'm in Iowa. I'll be back tomorrow.

> **DAD**
> Fine. Tomorrow then. 5:00. Don't be late.

I don't bother replying, since it isn't a question. It's a command. I mute notifications and put in my earbuds so I can ignore my life for the next twenty hours.

THIRTEEN

palmer

CHARLIE INVITED me out for Monday evening and seemed disappointed I had to decline. He offered to come over after I returned from my parents', but I didn't know how late I'd be nor was I all that sure I'd be in the mood. I appreciate how gracious he was, unlike Brennan, who threw a tantrum when he didn't get his way. The more I learn about Charlie, the more I wonder how I ever thought I loved a guy like Brennan. I must've been insane.

I show up at my parents' house just before five, wearing a floral jumper my mother had bought me. The wide legs and tapered waist aren't the most flattering to my frame, but the halter style of the top makes the girls look high and proud. Maybe wearing it will appease her enough she'll cut me some slack about whatever this meal is about. Probably more haranguing about Brennan. As a bonus, the jumper is long pants. I've picked up a few more ugly bruises since Jewel nailed me in practice a couple of weeks ago, and I definitely do not need my mother cueing in on those to add to her arsenal of criticisms.

I use the gate to let myself into the backyard and enter

through the back door, which leads me into a mudroom larger than my apartment's bedroom. Through there, I cross into the kitchen and inhale the sumptuous scent of lemon and basil. Our housekeeper and cook, Helen, stands at the oven stirring a pot. She turns her head and smiles when I enter. "Palmer, so lovely to see you."

"Thanks, Helen. You, too. What is this wonderful feast you're whipping up?" I walk over to the stove to take a peek.

"Lemon-Basil Salmon with a side of citrus-honey carrots, herbed rice pilaf, and a simple Caesar salad."

"It smells so good." I inhale deeply. "Why are you still working for my parents? You could open your own catering business or even a food truck."

She barks a sharp laugh. "At my age? No, thank you. After thirty years, I've grown accustomed to your parents' ways. I don't want to have to learn how to handle other customers."

"Twenty-eight years and I'm still trying to learn how to handle them." I kiss her cheek. "If you ever want to run away, my couch is a pull-out. I'll give you the bedroom."

"If I run away, darling, it'll be south to the Caribbean. Not Baltimore. No offense."

"None taken." I steal a crouton and pop it in my mouth, dodging Helen's playful smack. "Where are the folks, anyway?"

"In the parlor with the other guests."

I raise my eyebrows. "Other guests? They didn't tell me it was a dinner party."

Helen twists her lips into a sympathetic frown. "Good luck in there. Remember to hold your head high and your ground firm."

Helen understands how it is for me and has been a much-needed ballast of support growing up. She's the one who encouraged me to continue pursuing my sport against my parents' objections. I nod and roll my shoulders, cracking my neck side to side as I walk in the direction of the parlor toward the front of the house. I don't know what awaits me, but I'll have my game face on for it.

I stroll into the parlor where my parents each sit in matching ivory upholstered wingback chairs. Across from them, a couple about their age sits on the matching sofa, while next to them is a younger man who looks to be in his twenties, clean-shaven with short sandy hair styled conservatively and twinkling green eyes that mirror the woman's. A smattering of golden freckles dusts his nose. He stands when he notices me and offers a smile, drawing everyone's attention to the doorway.

"Palmer, you made it," my mother says, glancing at her watch. *And on time, Mother.*

My father and the other man rise from their seats. Dad greets me with a kiss on the cheek and ushers me into the room. "Palmer, these are the Frankels. Patsy, Ned—this is my daughter, Palmer. And this," he gestures to the young man, who reaches out a hand to shake mine, "is their son, Boone."

I shake Boone's hand, then his father's, and smile politely at Mrs. Wainwright. "Nice to meet you."

"The Wainwrights are new clients at the firm," my father explains, resuming his seat. Ned and Boone wait until I sit down in one of the Queen Ann chairs flanking the couch before they sit. "We're going to be helping them open a new 1,100-home community on the western end of the county."

"We're excited to start work later this summer," Mr. Wainwright adds.

"The Wainwrights are from Cumberland County," my mother explains. "Boone, here, will be overseeing the project on his father's behalf for the next eighteen months. I told him since you are about the same age, you could show him where all the young people go to have fun."

I'm caught off guard. Is my mother trying to fix me up with their clients' son? I force a smile, clenching my teeth together. "Since I live in Baltimore, that might be difficult. But I'd be happy to show you around there any time."

"You don't have to feel obligated," Boone says.

"She doesn't mind," my mother says, waving her hand. "She has plenty of time."

"In the off-season," I allow, even though I keep busy with youth coaching or speaking gigs, or playing the occasional international tournament.

"Off-season?" Boone asks. "What is it you do?"

"I play for the Baltimore Battle in the Women's Major League Lacrosse League."

Boone's face lights up. "Really? That is so cool. I was a middie in college. What position?"

"Goalie." I start to relax. Boone appears genuinely interested and talking about the game with people who care always puts me at ease.

"Sounds exciting," Mrs. Wainwright says. "Elaine, you never said your daughter is a professional athlete. I played competitive tennis in college, but I wasn't quite good enough to go pro."

"Very impressive," Mr. Wainwright agrees. He smiles at my parents. "You must be so proud. I'm surprised, Jeff, that wasn't the first thing out of your mouth when we first met. Boone graduated Summa Cum Laude from Wharton six years ago and I still have trouble resisting the urge to bring it up."

"Dad." Boone's cheeks flush, and I decide right then I like him. His humility isn't an act, unlike so many others.

"We're very proud of Palmer," my father says, looking at me so adoringly and so convincingly I believe him for a second.

"Dinner's ready," Helen announces into the room.

"Shall we?" Everyone stands as my father motions toward the door. I fall into step next to Boone while our parents each pair up to continue their conversations.

"I would really like to hear more about your team," Boone says.

"I don't know," I joke. "Once you get me started, it's hard to shut me up. I'm pretty passionate about my sport."

"Passion is a good thing," Boone says. "A famous philosopher once said, 'Nothing is as important as passion. No matter what you want to do with your life, be passionate.'"

I turn it over in my head. "Sounds wise. Plato? Gibran?"

"Bon Jovi," he answers with a straight face. I burst out laughing, earning a wide-eyed reprimand from my mother. Yep. I definitely like this guy.

FOURTEEN

palmer

DINNER WENT SO MUCH BETTER than I
could've hoped for, thanks to Boone and his parents. They
showed enough interest in me to keep my mother too
distracted to point out my flaws, along with suggestions for
improvement, of course. Boone's presence obviously affected
my parents in a positive way. I could already see the wedding
bells dancing in my mother's eyes, little bags of money
dancing in my father's as he no doubt calculated what a
merger between our families would be worth. The investment
bankers and the developers. But Boone's presence was also a
pleasant surprise for me. Conversation never waned and the
evening ended with me offering tickets for a home game anytime he wanted and Boone accepting.

I want to leave with the Wainwrights, but my parents ask
me to stay back a few minutes. My earlier optimism gives way
to a pit of dread in my stomach. I join my parents in the
kitchen, where my mother fills a kettle with water for tea and
my father uncaps a beer. I sit on a stool at the breakfast bar, playing with the tab of a can of Clearly Canadian.

Peach, my favorite. I'll have to thank Helen next time I see her for stocking it in the fridge for me.

"So," my mother begins. "What did you think of Boone?"

I roll my eyes. "He's very friendly. But I hope this wasn't supposed to be an attempt at matchmaking. I'm not ready to jump into something."

My mother clicks her tongue. "The best way to get over a bad fall is to get right back up on that horse."

I snort. "That's kind of what Tisha said."

"She sounds very smart." The kettle whistles. She removes it from the burner and pours the scalding liquid into her cup. "It's sad things didn't work out with Brennan. But now you can take what you learned from that failure and apply it to your next try. With Boone, perhaps?"

"Mom," I sigh.

"Oh, lay off her, Elaine," my dad sighs. He waves the bottle in the air. "Boone seems like a fine young man, but if Palmer isn't interested right now, it's understandable."

My mother dunks her tea bag a few times, then tosses it in the trash. "She's not getting any younger, and she's already wasted all those years with Brennan."

"I'm not even thirty yet, Mom," I protest.

"That's why it's time for you to get serious about settling down." She points at me with her cup. "Did you know your egg count will drop to only 100,000 by the time you're thirty? And when you reach thirty-five, it drops to just 25,000? After that, each year, there is a rapid decline in your fertility. These are your prime years, and you're wasting them playing that silly game."

"Elaine," my father warns.

I push my sparkling water aside and hop off the stool. "Ohh-kayyy. Time for me to go home. Thanks for dinner."

I bend to give my mother a perfunctory peck on the cheek and reach up to do the same with my dad. "Text me you got home safe," he reminds me.

I give him a thumbs up and hurry through the mudroom and out the back door. Only once I'm in my car and on 70 east headed back to Baltimore do I release my pent-up scream. It had been a rarely pleasant night, but my mother couldn't stand not leaving me with a parting shot. The reminder of my fertility had been harsh, even if she did have a point. I only have a couple of years before I hit my thirties. And what am I doing? Messing around with someone I don't have a future with instead of pursuing a real prospect. I look at my phone. Boone had given me his number. I could invite him to the next game. We could go to dinner. Maybe I'd drive down to Frederick on one of my days off, and we could picnic up at Gambrill or hike the Appalachian Trail.

And then what, Palmer? Ask him to move in? Pick out paint swatches and baby names? Until, like Brennan, he finally realizes he can do better?

"No." I slam my hand on the steering wheel. Boone may end up being The One, who knows? But if I date him now, I'll probably fall for him and end up repeating the same pattern. Then where does that leave me? Alone, again, and with a hell of a lot fewer eggs. Damn my mother for getting into my head.

I'm sticking with the plan for now. Charlie may not be able to give me a future, but he sure as hell can give me some orgasms, which is what I need right now.

It's just going on ten o'clock when I arrive home. I kick off my pumps and drop my purse and keys by the door, then dash off a quick text to let Dad know I made it home okay. My phone chirps with an incoming message. But it isn't Dad. It's Charlie.

CHARLIE
Are you home?

ME
Just got in. I was getting ready for bed.

CHARLIE
Want some help? 😏

I bite my lip, unsure if he's teasing me or if it's a genuine proposition. I type back "sure" and wait for his reply.

CHARLIE
Don't say it unless you mean it, Coco

ME
Coco? And do YOU mean it?

CHARLIE
Palmer=🌴=🥥=Coco

CHARLIE
I always mean what I say

ME
Then I'll wait for you. Park in the garage and you can come right up on the elevator.

CHARLIE
Be there in a few

I scramble to brush my teeth and fix my hair, then run through the apartment to make sure I haven't left anything embarrassing lying about. I've just finished when there is a knock on my door. After checking the peephole first, I open the door to a rumpled smokeshow of a man. Charlie isn't in his usual khakis and collared shirt, which he fills out nicely. Tonight, he's wearing a fitted black T-shirt with the Maryland flag and Baltimore Battle emblazoned across the chest, hanging loose over a pair of charcoal gray basketball shorts. His hair is mussed, a few stray pieces sticking up at odd angles like he'd just rolled out of bed. The dark shadow along his jawline is also new; Charlie always came to work with a smooth face. But I like this version of him. Very much.

"Are you going to let me in?" he asks, one corner of his lips tugging upward in a knowing smirk.

I clear my throat. "Of course."

I step back to let him enter, then shut and bolted the door. I turn around and lean against it with my hands behind my back, suddenly nervous. "How about a drink? I have a half-bottle of Shiraz, Cherry Cola, or water."

He scrutinizes me, rubbing his stubble as if deep in thought. "I'm supposed to be helping you to bed, so Cherry Cola would be counterintuitive."

He steps closer, into my personal space, and breathes deeply. "Minty, which means you already brushed?" I nod.

"Then that rules out wine. Have you ever had red wine after brushing your teeth?" He cringes. "As bad as drinking orange juice."

I lick my lips. "The drink is for you, not me."

He rubs his thumb against his lips. "I don't need a drink. At least not yet. Maybe after I've eaten."

I start. "Oh, sorry. It's so late, I didn't think to ask. I try to avoid junk food during the season, but I have plenty of fruits and veggies if you want a snack. Or I can make you a sandwich."

I start to move past him toward the kitchen, but he grasps my wrist and pulls me to a stop. "No, Coco. I don't want you to make me something to eat. *You* are my something to eat. Consider this lesson two."

charlie

I LOVE how lust-hazy her eyes are. I yank her into my body so she can feel how hard I am for her. It's been two days since I saw her last. Her squeak stokes the already simmering fire inside. She tilts her head up, offering me her parted lips. I lick into her mouth, savoring the cool mint of her tongue, grunting as she rubs against me. I pull away to ask where the bedroom is.

"Down the hall," she says, nodding her chin behind me.

Still holding her wrist, I pull her behind me past a bathroom and closet to a room with a door slightly ajar. I push it open and walk in, pleased to find it holds a king-sized bed. I like having room to maneuver, although for tonight's purposes, I only need Palmer to lie in one spot. Tonight is about worshipping her tight little pussy, undoing the damage her exes did. I need to show her how much I love her flavor. The sample I had the other night when she came all over my fingers triggered a craving for her I haven't been able to shake. Watching her come apart by my hand has been playing on a loop all weekend, so much so I had to buy a new bottle of lotion for the bedroom. I can't wait to sink my cock into all that wet heat. But first, I'm going to show her how good it can be with my tongue.

I spin her into the room and push her toward the bed. She starts to sit on the ivory duvet, but I shake my finger at her. "Can't climb into bed wearing street clothes. Wouldn't be very comfortable."

I turn her to face the bed, appreciating the bare span of her upper back. I undo the bow tied around her neck and slowly drag the hidden zipper down to her ass. She wears a rose pink strapless bra and I can't wait to see if her panties match. I slip my hands into the one-piece outfit on either side of her thighs and, with her help, carefully shimmy it over her hips and down her legs, following the fabric to my knees.

Sheer panties in a matching pink. Her ass is fantastic in them. I can't resist a bite.

She gasps and looks down over her shoulder at me, her eyes wide and sparkling. I smirk up at her and wink. "Couldn't resist."

She tries to turn, but I grip her hips to hold her in place. "Not yet, Coco. Let me admire you."

I glide my hand over the silky material covering her ass, moving between her legs to cup the apex of her thighs. Her wetness is evident through the sheer fabric. "So wet. Is that all for me, baby?"

"Yes," she whimpers, squirming.

I slide my hand out from between her legs and chuckle at her frustrated sigh. "Lift your leg, sweetcheeks. Gotta move these clothes out of the way."

She lifts first one then the other leg, allowing me to strip the outfit away and toss it to the side. Hands on hips, I turn her to face me, putting her pussy in my direct line of sight. She threads her fingers in my hair, steadying herself while I pull her panties down.

"Oh, Coco," I murmur, staring at the purple and yellow bruises on the front of both her upper thighs. I placed a kiss on a small cut across her kneecap. "Do they hurt?"

"Not anymore," she breathes. She kicks her underwear away, exposing the tight triangle of curls covering her mons.

"I'll be gentle," I promise, kissing each of her bruises as I travel up her legs until I reach the summit. I flick my tongue over her hooded bud, eliciting another whimper followed by a shiver.

"Sit down." She does as I command, which is hotter than Acapulco in August. "Good girl. Now take off your bra."

Without breaking eye contact, she reaches behind her and, in one move, flings the garment across the room. My mouth waters at the gorgeous sight in front of me. The other night, I'd gotten a glimpse of what she hid beneath her uniform, but here was the whole package. I have to touch her peachy skin, a sharp contrast to my own umber coloring, which will only darken as the summer wears on. Her tits are magnificent—rounded and large enough to spill over my hands as I palm them, testing their weight as I squeeze and massage. Her chest rising faster, her pink lips part as she watches me handle her. I catch her eye and pinch one rosy tip, calling forth a hiss as she tips her head back. Her hands find their way into my hair again and I let her tug me to those swells, knowing what she wants, what she needs. I'm going to drive her insane in just a few minutes, in my own way, so I acquiesce to this one demand of hers.

I clamp my mouth over one delicious tit and suck, hard, drawing her hard peak between my teeth. She writhes against me, quiet mewling sounds falling from her lips. I switch to her other mound and repeat myself, sucking, nipping, laving.

My breaths are ragged as I pull my head back, my cock pulsing against my shorts. Gently, I urge her to lie down, and like the good girl she is, she follows my direction. I hook my hands behind her knees and, careful to avoid her bruises, yank her forward until her ass is on the edge. She yelps, and I freeze. "Did I hurt you?"

"No, j-just surprised m-me," she stammers in an unsteady voice.

I bend forward and kiss her stomach, smiling at the tiny quake that shudders through her. "Spread your legs for me, Coco."

She doesn't move right away, so I urge her in a soothing voice. "Baby, I promise this will be so good for us."

After a brief hesitation, she draws in a deep breath and moves her legs apart, showing me her glistening pink petals. I have to close my eyes and talk my dick down before I come in my shorts like a teenager from only looking at her. "So fucking beautiful. Just lie back and enjoy. I'm about to show you how a goddess like you should be treated."

I caress the inside of her thighs and lean in to lick a path from her opening up to her clit, circling my tongue around the sensitive nub. I use my shoulders to hold her wide open for me, breathing in her sweet, tangy scent before plunging my tongue between the velvety lips of her sex. I thrust in and out in a steady rhythm, a preview of what will come when it's time to give her my cock. I flick faster as she keens and wriggles underneath me, using the tip of my nose to rub against her clit. I grab my cock in one hand while I replace my tongue with two fingers, moving up to suck her clit. High-pitched cries tell me she's getting close, her body vibrating as if connected to an electrical current. Her pussy, so slick with my saliva and her arousal, stretches to allow me to push in a third finger while I alternated between sucking on her clit and licking a circle around it. I found a good rhythm—in, out, circle, suck— increasing the pace as her walls tighten around my fingers.

A stream of curses bounce around the room, followed by a shout quickly muffled when she clamps her thighs to my head, her channel spasming around me as I suck hard on her clit. Not wanting to miss it, I move my tongue to her opening and work her nub with my thumb. She rubs her pussy against my face, a stream of creamy, sweet cum coating my tongue as her whole body arches. I squeeze my cock, trying desperately not to cum all over myself, but it's a battle I fear I'm losing.

Her thighs relax, her body trembling from the aftershocks of her orgasm. I lick her once more before standing.

"Baby, you're so fucking hot. You taste so good." I pull down my shorts, watching her eyes dilate as my cock springs free. I grip it in my palm and stroke hard, squeezing a drop of precum out of the tip. "Look what you do to me."

She sits up on her elbows and stares, transfixed, as my hand moves up and down my shaft. "I'm going to come all over you, okay?"

My heart drops when she shakes her head, but then she sits up and grasps my balls in her hand. "Come *in* me. You tasted me. Let me taste you."

I'm too far gone to argue. I let her take hold of my cock and wrap her lips around it while I grab her hair. "It's not going to take much."

And it doesn't. She squeezes my balls, sucking my length into her mouth, and that's it. Pulling on her hair, I empty myself down her throat, amazed at how she keeps sucking and swallowing as I jerk in her mouth. Black dots swim in front of my eyes as pleasure rips through me. Her dick of an ex didn't like this? Definitely a him problem, not a her problem.

I groaned, tipping my head back as the last of my cum spilled down her throat. My legs shake as I release her hair. She pops off me with an audible sound and I collapse to my knees, panting. The only sound is our heavy breaths mingling in the air. Then a chuckle turns into a giggle, and Palmer is leaning up on her elbows again, looking down on me with a smile that can outshine a million suns.

"What's so funny?" I wheeze. I draw in a steadying breath and let out a slow exhale in an attempt to calm my racing pulse.

"Not funny," she says on a sigh. "Laughing at how amazing that was. I never knew it could be so fucking good."

I pull my shorts back up and sit up on my knees, positioning myself between her legs. She leverages herself up, and when she's close enough, I put my hand on the back of her head and pull her lips to mine. I take her mouth deep, my tongue sliding against hers, our musk comingling. When we separate, her eyes roam my face, a small crease forming between her brow but disappearing before I could make sense of it. Is she confused? Regretful?

I don't get a chance to ask before she pushes me away and hops off the bed. "Last one in the shower is a rotten egg."

I grin and give chase, my heart flipping in my chest.

SIXTEEN

THE NEXT COUPLE of weeks pass like a rip shot. My days are all lacrosse—practices, games, and meetings. My nights are all Charlie. He'd come over with takeout and we'd enjoy a friendly dinner, sitting next to one another on the couch, talking about everything and anything. We still haven't had intercourse yet, and it's driving me mad. But Charlie has shown me all the different ways one can be pleased, and provide pleasure, with just a few fingers, lips, and a tongue. Nothing has topped the first night, though. After we'd showered, he went down on me twice more. I'd never come so much and so hard. When this was over, I'd have a hell of a time finding anyone like him. He might be in danger of ruining me.

I frown, the thought of things ending crashing my mood. But it will end. Charlie doesn't do commitment, I keep reminding myself. And I need to learn how to do chill and casual, instead of jumping from one serious relationship to another. Getting attached wouldn't be good for either of us, especially me.

"What's that look for?" Tisha whispers, elbowing me. We're sitting in the conference room watching game film of our biggest competitor, and my former team, the Philadelphia Stars. "We're on a streak, while Philly's already lost two."

"It's nothing," I whisper back, keeping my eyes on the film even though my attention is somewhere else. In a certain office about three floors up.

"Right." Tisha turns her attention back to the film, but taps my notebook with her pen.

I look down at the page. I'm supposed to be taking notes, but I've been doodling. Worse, I've written out Charlie's name and surrounded it with flourishes, like some lovesick thirteen-year-old. I scratch it out and flip the page, drawing a few stares from the sudden action. Coach Kayla, who'd been pointing out key moments in the film, paused and raised her brows at me.

"Sorry," I mutter. Coach continues, and I do my best to focus the rest of the time.

After, a few of the defensive players fall in step with Tisha and me, cutting off her opportunity to quiz me about Charlie, something she's probably dying to do. "Since practice doesn't start until after noon tomorrow, we're going to Poe's tonight," Vera says, gesturing to my other teammates. "Y'all want to join?"

"I'd love to, but Manny and I have plans," Tisha says.

Charlie and I didn't have solid plans, though he's slept over almost every night, leaving early in the morning to go home and change. I want to hang out with him, but maybe a little space will be good. This thing between us needs to breathe.

"Yeah, I'll be there."

"Cool," Vera says. "Happy Hour starts at five, but most of us aren't getting there until later."

Tisha and I walk in the opposite direction. We stop next to my car and I throw my bag in the backseat. Tisha is bouncing on the soles of her feet, her eyes bright with excitement. "Sooo —you haven't given me an update in a week."

"You have a hunky husband." I chuckle. "You don't need to live vicariously through me."

She clucks her tongue. "It's not living vicariously. It's being thrilled my good friend is finally getting good D. We can trade stories."

I wrinkle my nose. "We've talked about sex before."

"Yeah, but I held back." Tisha fixes the headband holding back her locs. "I didn't want to make you feel bad going on and on about Manny's prowess while you were trying to find a good vibrator to get you off since Brennan wasn't doin' the job."

A flush crawls up my neck and settles in my cheeks. I put my hands to them, their heat obvious under my palms. "I was so pathetic. I can't believe I settled for *meh*."

Tisha pulls my hands from my face and squeezes my wrists. "You're not pathetic. You're sweet and kind and loyal. But none of it matters now because you have a man who's treating you the right way. He is, right? I don't have to take a long pole to his kneecaps?"

I sigh. "He treats me like a goddess, T. And to be truthful, it's a bit of a problem."

"How in the world is being treated so well a problem?"

"Because," I hedge, looking down, my cheeks still hot. "I keep forgetting this is only temporary. I'm going to fail my experiment if this keeps up."

Tisha settles back against her car, her fuchsia-stained lips pursed. "Why?"

I scoff. "Why do I keep forgetting? Because I've never felt as good as I feel when I'm with him. And it's not only the sex, which, by the way, is still in the oral stages."

Tisha's eyes widen. "He hasn't slipped the magic sausage to you?"

"No, and," I faux-gag, "Please never say that again."

Tisha snort-laughs. "No, I mean why does it have to be temporary?"

I stare at her in astonishment. "You know why. I need to break my serial monogamy habit, remember?"

"Yeahhh," Tisha drags out the word. "However—"

"'However' what?"

She flips her hair over her shoulder. "I'm just sayin', he treats you like gold, gives you the best orgasms of your life with no expectation in return, he respects your job, he's hot—he's like the unicorn of boyfriends."

"Except for the part where he doesn't do commitment and has a different woman on his arm every week."

"Yeah, except for that." Tisha unlocks her car and puts her bag on the seat. "Have fun tonight. But pencil me in for some girl time this weekend. We've got a lot to talk about."

The whole way home, I think about what Tisha said. Charlie *is* acting like the perfect boyfriend, which is a problem. Because while he is having fun pretending, it's becoming all too real to me.

I walk into Poe's a little after eight to find most of my team and several of the front office staff occupying various tables and barstools. I wave hi to the media team sitting at the same table as last time, noting Charlie isn't among them, and make my way to where Marisol, Vera, Andi, Jewel, and a few other women sit laughing. Colorful drinks in oversized cocktail glasses dot the table, which they pick up and toast her with when she approaches.

"Goalie's in the house!" shouts Marisol.

"First round's on the Captain," Vera says, motioning to the bar where Ava sits with her husband, JJ Jennings. JJ and Ava had grown up together and were reunited a few years back when JJ was traded from the Memphis Ducks to the Red Hawks for what would end up as his last season. I'd heard the story of how JJ had once broken Ava's heart, but after being forced together for publicity purposes and having to pretend they got along, they'd healed their rift. They'd married a little more than a year ago in a small outdoor ceremony I'd attended.

"Glad you could come out," Ava says, pulling me into a hug. "Order anything you want. JJ's paying."

JJ winks at his wife. "Anything for my love."

"You guys are too sweet," I sigh.

"Sickening, right?"

Charlie's breath ghosts across the back of my neck, raising goosebumps over my flesh. I turn, my breasts brushing his chest. A flame sparks in his eyes at the contact, and my nipples become obvious peaks under the thin Kermit the Frog crop top I'm wearing. He glances down and the quick flick of his tongue across his lips is a zap to my center.

"Hey," I say, my voice sounding ridiculously breathy to me. I clear my throat and try again. "Hi."

I move to the side, putting a few inches between us. Charlie quirks a brow and gives me an amused grin before acknowledging Ava and JJ. "How's married life treating you?"

"Every day's a honeymoon," JJ answers, his arm draped around Ava's bare shoulders. She's wearing a racerback tank-style dress that draws attention to the muscles in her arms and back. I'd kill to pull off a look like that, but my shoulders were too wide to look cute in that kind of outfit.

I lift my finger to catch the bartender's attention. "I'll have one of those cocktails my friends are drinking." I point toward the table.

"Rum punch?" she asks. "Sure. Guava, Orange, Pineapple, or Passionfruit juice?"

"Passionfruit," Charlie answers for me. The bartender raises a pierced brow and looks to me for confirmation. I nod.

She jerks her chin at Charlie. "What would you like?"

"Guinness Blonde, draft, please."

The bartender moves away to pour our drinks. "Palmer, I've been meaning to tell you," Ava says. "You're doing a hell of a job in goal this season."

My heart does a happy dance. "Thank you. No one will ever replace Tisha, but I'm happy to be doing my part for the team."

"Tisha's great," Ava agrees. "But so are you. You have what it takes to be a real franchise player. I'm glad we were able to talk Philly into trading you."

"Me, too," I laugh.

"Me, three," adds Charlie. He puts a hand on my lower back, his fingers cool on the heated skin between the hem of my shirt and the waistband of my pleated skirt. He touches me with light strokes, his fingers edging lower. I want to melt into him, encourage him to feel the lack of barrier between the soft cotton and my ass. But so many people are around. He has to stop touching me like this before someone notices. I stiffen, and Charlie stops his caress, but locks his hand firmly around my waist.

"Charlie, you keeping up with the Red Hawks?" JJ asks, seemingly oblivious to the tension between Charlie and me. I can barely breathe with him so close, it's amazing no one else seems to notice.

"Of course," Charlie says. He and JJ launch into a conversation about the Hawks' new lineup and how far they could expect to go. My heart pounding in my ears drowns out most of the noise and I'm relieved when the bartender puts our drinks in front of us.

"Thanks for the round, Ava." I salute my captain with the large glass, grateful for the cool condensation. "I'm going to sit with the girls. Talk to you all later."

I scoot past Charlie, who barely moves so I have to brush against him again. The smirk on his face confirms he's teasing. I shoot him a look I hope he takes as a warning. Payback can be a bitch and the next time I get him alone, I'll show him exactly how much.

SEVENTEEN

"IS something going on with you and Charlie?" Jewel whispers in my ear.

I choke on the Dr. Pepper I'd just sipped. I'd switched to soda after the giant punch cocktail had the room spinning. Now I have only a pleasant buzz going, but Jewel's question almost sobers me completely.

"Why do you ask?" I say, hoping I sound nonchalant and not panicked. Fat chance, but I can hope.

"Because he hasn't stopped looking at you all night." She gestures with the plastic sword that came in the cocktail between me and Charlie, who is two tables away. "And I know you noticed because you've been looking over there almost the whole time."

I take another sip of Dr. Pepper to buy myself time. "If I'm staring at him, it's because he's hot. I mean, look at him, right? But I doubt he's staring at me. He's probably checking out the women at the bar behind me." I wave in that general direction.

Jewel narrows her eyes. "Uh-huh, I see. So nothing going on."

"That's right. We're only friends."

"Well, I never had a friend who looked at me like he wanted to take me to a dark corner and devour me. But I'm from a little town in Pennsylvania, so maybe it's a city thing. Like those peppermint sticks stuck in lemon wedges."

"Those are so good," I say, suddenly wanting one. I'd never heard of those until Brennan and I visited the traditional Flower Mart downtown a couple of years ago. If I remember this tomorrow, I'll add lemons and peppermint sticks to my shopping list.

"If you say so," Jewel snorts. She turns her face toward me and hides her mouth. "Don't look now, but your hot friend is heading this way."

I'm about to protest, but then Charlie appears at the table. My teammates greet him with a synchronized chorus of "Hi, Charlie!", drawing attention to us.

"Hello, ladies. Having a good time?" he asks. He makes small talk with everyone at the table, and I begin to relax, since it no longer seems obvious he came over just for me. But then, he turns his dimples on me.

"Hey, Palmer. Can I speak to you for a minute, in private?" He nods toward a door leading to the back hallway of the bar, which leads to the bathrooms and the back alley.

"Um, sure." I hop off my stool and grasp the table for balance. The buzz is still rolling strong through me. Charlie puts his hand under my elbow to steady me and holds onto it as he guides me to the back. Once we push through the swinging door and turn the corner, we're out of sight of the main bar area.

"What did you want to—oomph—"

I'm cut short by Charlie's mouth on mine. He backs me against the wall and claims my lips in a passionate, punishing kiss. Once the initial shock wears off, I melt into it, wrapping my hands around his head as he plunders my mouth. Soft sighs are met with deep grunts. In my heels, we're about the same height. He puts a hand under my thigh and hooks my leg over one of his hips, perfectly aligning us. I moan when his hard steel makes contact with my bare heat. His hand glides up my thigh to my bare ass, then follows a path in my crease.

"Fuck," he murmurs against my mouth. "Are you bare?"

"Surprise." My giggle morphs into a low gasp when the tip of his finger presses against my rear entrance. He chuckles lightly at my shock.

"Tease me, I tease you," he growls. He rubs against me, holding his finger in place between my cheeks. I wheeze, my breath catching partly from nerves, partly from arousal. "Don't worry, we aren't here yet."

He applies a little more pressure, then removes his hand and smacks my buttocks. "But we'll get there someday."

I whimper, desperate need blazing from my core outward. I crush my lips against his, stroking and sucking his tongue, taking what I want. His other hand reaches under my skirt and skims across my slit. Before I can encourage him to go farther, we hear footsteps and untangle ourselves in time for the door to swing inward. Charlie turns his back so his tented pants aren't visible, resting an arm against the wall to block most of my body from sight.

"Oh, sorry," a woman's voice sings out, followed by a snicker. I peer over Charlie's shoulder to see Mei and Liberty walking into the restroom. Liberty has a strange look on her face when she catches my eye, but she quickly glances away.

"It was Mei and Liberty." I groan, dropping my face into my hands. "We look so obvious."

"Is it really that big a deal?" Charlie huffs.

I look up at his scowling face, though he looks more hurt than angry. "I guess not. I just didn't want anyone to know we were hooking up."

A muscle tics in Charlie's cheek. "Are you embarrassed?"

"God, no," I insist. "If anything, it'd be the opposite. I'm not exactly your type."

He runs his hands through his hair and huffs. "My type," he mutters.

His eyes roam over my features. Does he see what I see, the moon face and apple-round cheeks? Pale, blotchy skin made worse when I was embarrassed? The unusual eyes, the nose slightly too wide, and the mouth that always felt too large?

"I wish you'd believe how beautiful you are. I want people to know we're together because I feel so fucking lucky." His voice hitches and he clears his throat. "Coco, I need to tell you—"

The door to the women's restroom bangs open, making us both jump. Charlie lets go of my cheek as Liberty stomps away, followed a minute later by Mei, who gives us a wink and a sly smile. Charlie drops his head on a sigh. "Sorry. I should go and let you finish the night with your friends."

"Charlie, don't go," I put a hand on his chest. "I feel lucky to be with you, too."

He gives me a half-smile and kisses me quick on the lips. "Have fun tonight and we'll talk tomorrow, 'k?"

My shoulders slump, but I agree and he holds my hand for another moment before exiting out the alleyway door. I use the restroom to put myself back together—smooth my hair down, fix my smeared lip gloss. Then I rejoin my teammates, ignoring their loaded questions and changing the subject until they finally move on to different topics. I can't focus, though, my mind drifting back to Charlie.

I wish you'd believe how beautiful you are. I want people to know we're together because I feel so fucking lucky.

Did he really mean that? It's been more than two weeks since we made our arrangement, and I could think of a million

96

ways he's made me feel special. More than that, he's made me feel treasured, something no one—not my parents, not my previous boyfriends—has ever done. But is this why he's so popular with women? Is this how he is with all of them?

I try to stay longer, but my thoughts won't stop straying to Charlie. I want to be with him. So I say my goodbyes and head out the door, debating whether I should warn him I'm on my way or simply show up and hope he lets me in.

I'm barely out the door when Liberty calls out to me. "Palmer, wait up."

I stop and wait for her, clocking her appearance. Her ruby locks, normally sleek and shiny, are a frizzy halo around her head. Her hazel-brown eyes are glassy, her lipstick smeared in one corner, and her cheeks have an alcohol flush to them. She walks unsteadily in her Steve Madden wedges. She is the picture of drunken regrets, and I feel sorry for her.

"Hey, Liberty. Do you need a lift somewhere?" I hold up my phone. "I can call a Lyft."

She dismisses me with a shaky wave of her hand. "Mei's taking me home. I wanted to tell you something."

"Okay." I shift on my feet, waiting for what I have a sneaking suspicion is going to be something about Charlie. I'm proven right.

"He'll break your heart," she says. "He's so good-looking. So charming. Says all the right things. But he'll never settle down."

I look around, but thankfully, it doesn't seem like anyone inside is paying attention to us. The last thing I want is a public argument with a drunken colleague. "Look, Liberty. I appreciate the warning, but it's not necessary. Charlie and I are friends—"

"Did he tell you how lucky he is to be with you? How he wishes you knew how beautiful and special you are?" Her lips curl in an ugly snarl. "He did. I can tell by your face. And you fell for it."

I refuse to admit anything to her, especially not that she's right. My heart drops to my feet. It shouldn't matter. He's not my boyfriend and he never will be. In fact, I'm happy Liberty tells me this because now it's easier to quash any growing feelings.

"Thank you," I say, clearing my throat. "I appreciate the heads up. But it's unnecessary, truly. Have a good night, Liberty."

I move down the block, checking once over my shoulder to ensure she went back inside. Around the corner, I lean against a building and blow out a breath. My plan to surprise Charlie at his place isn't a no-brainer any longer. I take out my phone and call up the rideshare app, dithering between following through or calling it and going home. Does what Liberty said change anything? So what if he uses the same lines; makes sense why he would switch women as often as he switches socks if he's got a standard repertoire he uses.

My finger hovers over the icon for the rideshare app. *Come on, Palmer. Make a decision. Go home or go to Charlie?*

I tap the screen and pocket my phone.

EIGHTEEN
charlie

I'VE SENT Palmer three texts with no response. Maybe she's pissed I left her at the bar and I wouldn't blame her. It was a chicken shit move on my part. I'm the one who kept pushing the line, who kept touching and flirting in front of everyone, who nearly fucked her against the wall in public despite her desire to keep things between us private. Of course she doesn't want everyone to know her business. I know my reputation, shit, I lean into it. Why would she want to risk her reputation among the team getting involved with a horny asshole like me?

Shit. I fucked up. I left her there to face the consequences of us getting caught, by Liberty of all people. If it were one of her teammates or anyone else in the office, there'd have been some snickers and teasing, I'm sure, and then everyone would have forgotten about it by next week. I don't trust Liberty, though. Especially after I've been denying anything going on between Palmer and me. Liberty will take that shit personally.

Matt's staying with my parents for a few days to help Dad out on a custom job, so I have the apartment to myself. I take a hot shower, finishing with a blast of cold water, grab a Natty

Boh from the fridge, and settle into my favorite corner of our leather sectional with the remote. I throw on the Top Gear channel and try to lose myself in the inanity of the original Clarkson, Hammond, and May trio. But my mind keeps going back to Palmer. Not only am I going to have to make up for tonight, I'm going to need to step up my game. It's hard during the season to plan around practices and games. The few days the players have off aren't enough to do something big, like fly her down to Mexico to meet my Abue and Abu. But I can bring Mexico to her. I'm checking the calendar for a good time to make her dinner when the doorbell rings.

I frown at the clock. No one comes over this late. I switch to the camera app and leap to my feet, rushing to the door.

"Hey," I say when I open the door.

"Hi." Palmer stands on the stoop, her hands fisted around the strap of the purse she wears across her chest. She cranes her neck to see behind me. "Is it okay if I come in?"

I find my voice and swing the door open. "Yeah, of course. Come in, come in."

She steps inside and does a small circle while I shut and bolt the door. I glance around, looking at the apartment through her eyes. Our place takes up the ground floor of a two-level townhome. Like Palmer's, there's only a square of entryway before you're in the living room, and I'm grateful Matt and I haven't left a mess lying around. Except for my can of beer resting in the cupholder of the pull-down armrest and a few pairs of sneakers kicked into the corner by the door, everything is tidy.

"It's nice," she remarks finally. She moves further into the room and notices the flatscreen taking up half a wall, the shelves underneath holding a video game console and an assortment of cartridges and accessories. Her eyes widen, amusement dancing in her eyes. "Definitely a bachelor pad."

"Oh, come on," I scoff. "I'm sure there are plenty of women with 100" plasma screens taking up most of their wall space."

"I'm sure there aren't," she says with a giggle. Her eyes drift to my bare chest and her throat works noticeably before she turns her attention elsewhere.

"Is your brother home?"

"No, he's in Annapolis for the weekend working with my dad." I gesture to the couch. "Have a seat. Can I get you a drink?"

She sits on the other side of the armrest and lifts my can. "National Bohemian? Really? You only ever drink import or craft beer when we go out."

I shrug. "Natty Boh's our comfort beer, what can I say? Always reliable. Want one?"

She grimaces. "I'm still feeling the cocktail from earlier. But water would be great."

I fetch her a glass with filtered ice water and take the seat next to her. "How was the rest of your night?"

She drinks half the water in one gulp before answering with a tiny shrug. "Fine."

"Did anyone give you a hard time?" I take a small sip of beer, watching her closely. There's a small flinch, but she gives a half-smile.

"A little teasing." She sets the glass down and removes her purse, resting it on the table.

"Palmer, I'm sorry." I put my beer on the table so I can raise the armrest and slide closer to her. "I shouldn't have put you in that position, and I really shouldn't have just left."

"It's okay."

"It's not," I stress. I put my arm on the cushion behind her and lean in, searching her eyes. "I should have respected your decision to keep things between us quiet."

"No, you're right," she says, dragging her hand down

my chest and scratching across my abs. My heart races and the lightweight gray sweats I'm wearing can't hide what the hungry expression on her face is doing to my cock.

"Who cares if people know, right? We're consenting adults having some fun." She licks her lips and stares up at me. "Right?"

I swallow back the fierce protest. I want to tell her no, it's not just some fun. Not for me. I catch the way she glances at me sometimes, and I believe it's not only about having a good time for her, either. There's something here, something more than chemistry, more than a simple spark.

But she isn't ready to hear it yet. She has a plan and it's too soon to sway her to make some changes. So all I can do is agree. "Right."

Her eyes travel over my chest and lower, flashing with heat when she reaches my thickening steel. She roams my face, biting her lip, begging me with a flick of her tongue across her bottom lip to kiss her. So I do. I take her face between my palms and slant my mouth over hers, giving gentle sipping kisses, the soft slide of my tongue between her lips neither desperate nor harsh. Exploring, tasting, deepening.

On a sigh, she pushes me away. "Can we move to your bedroom? It's my turn to explore all of you."

I stand and pull her up from the couch. Before she can protest, I bend and scoop her into my arms. Her mouth flops open, but she quickly recovers and hangs an arm around my neck for support. She takes off her shoes and lets them drop along the way.

"No one has ever carried me before," she says in wonder. "I'm too tall, too—"

"Shh." I peck her lips and march down the hall to my room. "You're too perfect. That's the only adjective I'll accept after the word 'too' when it comes to you. Besides, are you questioning my strength? I may not be a bodybuilder, but I can carry my girl."

Her cheeks pinken, but she doesn't say anything else. When we reach my room, I set her down on the edge of my bed and stand back, lifting my arms out to the side. "How do you want me?"

She bites her lip and grabs the waist of my sweats to tug me into her. I close my eyes as she licks around my belly button and places open-mouth kisses all along my abs. She lightly traces the tattoo inked on the left side of my ribcage, a purplish-blue passionflower, tickling a shiver up my spine before tracing the Mexican eagle tattooed on the right side of my ribs. She looks up at me through her lashes, arching one brow.

"One for my mother, one for my father," I rasp in reply to her silent question, my arousal growing heavier with every light pass of her fingertips over my skin. My head drops forward. I run my hands down her hair, the silky strands flowing through my fingers while she continues to explore with her lips and fingers, following the thin trail of hair leading into my pants. She eases them over my hips, freeing my pulsing steel, swirling her tongue and spreading the beaded precum around the head. My breaths turn ragged, my muscles straining from resisting the urge to push between her pillowy lips into her hot, wet mouth. When she wants me, she'll take me. This is her call tonight.

"Lie down," she commands in a soft but firm voice. I climb onto the bed next to her and lie on my back. My cock bobs against my stomach as she shifts on the bed, rising to her knees next to me and removing her top. Her chest heaves, those glorious tits rising and falling, and when she reaches behind to unclasp her bra, I bite my fist to stifle a groan as they fall free.

"Touch me."

She doesn't have to ask twice. I palm her mounds, her nipples already hard as I twist and pull them. She closes her eyes and moans, leaning over and bracing her hand on the pillow next to my head. I keep working one tit with my hand while I suck the other into my mouth, stroking her stiff peak with my tongue. I slide my free hand up her skirt, her arousal coating my fingers with a pass through her slick heat.

She answers with a deep groan and bucks against my hand. I take the hint and she's so wet it takes nothing to breach her entrance with my middle and ring finger. I press the heel of my palm against her bud while I curl my digits, looking for the button that makes her scream. I pinch her tit and suck her swollen nipples. It's not long before her pussy clenches around me, her keening turning into loud, long moans until at last she detonates around me, screaming my name along with a litany of pleas to every known God and Goddess in existence.

She collapses, quivering and boneless, on top of me. I roll her under me and tug off her skirt, the breath knocked out of my lungs at the spectacular beauty before me.

Ivory skin glowing, lit only by the moonlight drifting in through the partially open blinds. She's fucking flawless. I pepper her face and neck with tiny kisses, my dick throbbing, weeping for release. But it'll be on her terms. Whatever she wants. I'm hers. Totally and completely hers.

"Coco," I say, my voice gravelly with desire. "What do you want? I'll do anything you want. Name it."

She caresses my jaw, her eyes twin blue flames. "Fuck me, Charlie. I want you to fuck me."

NINETEEN

palmer

CHARLIE'S golden brown eyes liquefy into molten pools transfixed on my face. A pulse ticks in his jaw as he rakes his gaze down my body, his brows lowering and lips spreading into a wolfish grin. A thrill of anticipation ripples through me. He leans down and presses a kiss to my stomach, then to each breast and my neck before sweeping his tongue along my lips. "Are you sure?"

I nod vigorously. My breathing has shallowed, my heart still galloping in my chest. He kisses a hot path back down my neck. "Do you," I swallow, "want to?"

He sits up and stares down at me with a mixture of perplexity and need. He pushes his hard-on against my leg. "Can't you tell? I want nothing more than to be inside you. I want to crawl inside your body, slip myself inside those velvet walls and feel you pulse around me, your sweet cunt milking my cock until I can't see anything but you coming apart under me, hear nothing but you screaming my name, feel nothing but you wrapped around me burning with pleasure, until we're both so consumed in the fire we won't know where we end and the other begins.

"So yes, Coco. I want to." He kisses the corner of my mouth. "I want this." He kisses the sensitive pearl under my tight curls.

"I want you." He kisses the top of my left breast. I melt like ice dropped on a city street in July.

He gathers me in his arms and kisses me like the world is ending—deep, desperate, and demanding. The mattress undulates as he continues to steal my breath, moving his way between my thighs to nestle against my bare flesh. He pauses long enough to reach into the drawer of the nightstand and remove a foil packet, tearing it open with his teeth before biting at my lips to let his tongue in again. There's more shifting until his hot length nudges my center. I drop my knees, opening myself to him. He releases my mouth and in unspoken synchronicity, we stare down as he fists the base of his sheathed cock and guides it to my entrance. In one smooth thrust, he rocks inside me. I swallow a gasp at how deep he fills me.

"Are you okay?" he whispers, watching my face with intense concern. He's holding still, the muscles in his arms quaking while he keeps himself propped above me, unmoving as I adjust to his girth.

"More than," I say on a catch of breath.

Slowly, he pulls out to the tip, then pushes back in with just as much care. It's like every nerve in my body is connected to the ones inside my sex, and as he drags his length against my inner walls, they all erupt in a series of tiny explosions, shooting out to my toes and the ends of my hair. I meet him thrust for thrust, gradually climbing to a steady pace. He changes the angle of his push with a tilt of my hips. I cry out as with each rock forward, he taps the deep well of hidden pleasure in me. In only a couple of weeks, I've experienced more pleasure, learned more about my own body than in ten years of sexual activity. Until Charlie, I thought the clit was my most sensitive part, and that a good vibrator or well-placed thumb were the only ways to unlock all its splendidness. I was wrong. So wrong. So so wrong...

Charlie picks up the tempo, and it's not long before I start floating. I'm only feeling and pleasure and stardust in his arms, as his dick taps, taps, taps its magic code against my pleasure center. Moans become cries become shouts while I beg him not to stop, don't stop, never ever stop.

"Charlie," I wail, digging my nails into his backside. "Charlie, God, Charlie."

"That's it, baby," he groans with me. "Take all of me like a good girl."

Sweat-soaked skin slaps together, and one minute I'm pinned to the bed under Charlie's body, the next I'm flying, flying, flying into the atmosphere. I burst into a million stars, shuddering, shaking, and gasping for air.

"Fuck. I'm coming, baby. God, you're so fucking hot. I can't stop." With a roar, Charlie takes off right behind me, lifting my leg to his shoulder to press even deeper into me. A second rocket, smaller but no less fiery, shoots off in me at the same time he pounds into me one final time. In a fit of convulsive thrusts, Charlie empties himself before collapsing to the side, gulping for air.

"Fuck," he moans, his face smothered in the sheets.

I can't speak, only gasp for oxygen as my senses slowly return to me. I've heard people talk of seeing heaven after good sex, but until now I couldn't imagine it. This is nirvana. Pure joy.

Charlie lifts his head, his breathing still ragged. He holds on to the end of the condom as he slides out of me. "Be right back. Let me take care of this."

He flips on the bedside light and gets up. I can barely move, every muscle in my body no stronger than Jello. Charlie returns with a warm, wet washcloth and with a tender touch cleans between my legs. "Can I get you some water?"

"Sure," I say, suddenly self-conscious.

Maybe Charlie senses this because he drapes the light blanket folded at the foot of his bed over me and kisses my cheek. "Will you stay the night?"

"Do you normally spend the night with your, um, dates?"

He shares a lopsided smile. "No, Palmer."

"Oh."

He makes a sound like a half-chuckle. "Yeah. *Oh.* But you can stay. I'm asking you to stay."

"Oh. Well. If you're asking," I say, trying to keep the moment light.

He kisses me quick. "Be right back."

While he's gone, I stare at the ceiling and think about what just happened. Not the sex. I don't need to think about that because it will forever be imprinted on my brain. What I wish I could figure out is why he wants me to stay and whether I should. If this is only a fling, I should find my clothes and slink back home, right? As unappealing as it sounds, it's probably the right move. We're friends, and he's probably only being polite. If I were some random woman, he'd probably have called me a Lyft already.

I slip out from under the blanket and stand, glad my legs are strong enough again to hold me up. He returns with two waters and frowns when he sees me. "You aren't staying?"

I'm about to explain it's better if I go home, but something in his eyes stops me. I shake my head. "Just need the bathroom."

"Oh." His relief is palpable. He hands me a glass and I greedily drink. "Across the hall."

"Thanks," I say, handing the glass back. When I'm finished, I come back to the bedroom to find he's turned the bed down and is lying on one side. He pats the empty space next to him and I climb in beside. He turns off the light and puts his arm around me.

We settle down, my head resting on his chest while he plays with my hair. "Your hair is so soft. It's like cornsilk."

"It's so fine," I say. "I wish I had some texture to it. I'm actually jealous of Tisha's locs."

"I don't know if you can pull off locs, Coco."

"Duh." I poke him in the side and he makes a good-natured grunt. "Though I always wanted pink highlights."

"Why don't you get them? What's stopping you?"

"Nothing now, I guess." He keeps playing with my hair while I lazily scratch his chest. "Did your tattoos hurt?"

"Yeah. The ribs are probably the most painful place to be inked, but once I got the first one, I was compelled to follow through and put the second one on the opposite side. My next one will be on my ass." His chest rumbles with laughter.

"So, fleshy parts are better?"

"Generally speaking. You thinking about getting a tattoo?"

"Maybe."

He chuckles. "Tattoos, pink hair. Are we going through a rebellious phase?"

"Maybe. But what do you think? Should I go for it?"

He's quiet for a moment. Then he says in a serious voice, "Palmer, if you want to dye your hair pink or get a tattoo, then do it. But only if you truly want it for yourself. Don't do it to get back at your mom or your ex or whoever. And don't do it to please anyone else. Okay?"

I choke down a bubble of emotion. "I promise."

His breath begins to even out, but his fingers still move in my hair, lulling me into a sense of peace. I think about being the exception to his rule regarding sleepovers and I wonder if Liberty was also an exception. But I can't ask. There is something, though, I have been curious about. "Charlie. Can I ask you something?"

"Anything," he murmurs.

"Have you ever been serious with anyone before? Or have you always been anti-commitment?"

His fingers stop moving, and when he doesn't say anything for a while, I assume he's not going to answer. But then he resumes his lazy caresses. "Once. Her name was Angela and I was planning on proposing to her after college graduation."

"What happened?"

"During spring midterms, I decided to skip study group and head back to my dorm to take a nap." He gives a humorless laugh. "Apparently, so did Angela. And my roommate, who was also my best friend. Only they weren't napping when I walked in."

I lift myself to look at him. He's in shadows, the moonlight only revealing a small portion of his face, but the heartbreak is hard to miss. "I'm so sorry, Charlie."

"Funny," he says, taking his eyes off me to stare at the ceiling. "That's exactly what she said."

"Hey." I tug on his chin so he's looking at me. "She's a total moron to have let you go and I hope—no, I *know*—she regrets losing you every day of her miserable life."

A small smile turns his mouth up. "You think so?"

"Yup." I kiss his jaw. "Because if a guy like you were in love with me and I did something stupid enough to make him leave, I'd spend the rest of my life in abject misery."

His mouth opens, then closes, and he swallows. He adjusts our positions so we're on our sides facing each other.

Worldessly, he kisses me so tenderly I can weep, and before I realize it, he's rolled protection on and is back inside of me. This time, he rocks me gently, quietly, until we're both too spent to do anything but fall asleep in each other's arms.

TWENTY

palmer

I'VE JUST FINISHED BACK-TO-BACK road games, and we have a rare weekend break when my mother summons me to the estate. It's Father's Day, and I'm hard-pressed to come up with an excuse to skip out on a barbecue for my dad without looking like a brat. Charlie is spending the weekend in Annapolis with his own dad, anyway, so now is as good a time as any to face my parents. Traffic into Frederick is slow, and I find my thoughts drifting to Charlie.

It's been two weeks since the first night we had sex, and since then, we've spent every night together except on road trips, where I shared a room with Tisha if Charlie accompanied us. I've been having the best games of my life and when I'm not playing or at practice, I'm with Charlie. Last week, he cooked me one of his Abue's recipes, and he introduced me to her over FaceTime when he had to call for some last-minute advice on seasoning. I also finally met his brother, Matt, who was just as handsome as Charlie. Unfortunately, I met him in the middle of the night when I went to the kitchen for a glass of water , wearing only one of Charlie's dress shirts. He was a gentleman, pretending not to notice while I scampered back to Charlie's room for a pair of shorts. I'm still a little mortified.

After practice the other day, Tisha asked me if I was abandoning my plan. "Meeting the family? Spending most of your time together? It's starting to sound like a commitment, not a fun fling."

"It may seem like it, but it's not," I assured her, retaping my stick on the sidelines. "In fact, it's going exactly to plan. Sure, I met his grandma and his brother, and yes, we're sharing a bed more often than not. But do you see me on Pinterest looking for wedding party ideas or bookmarking baby names? No, you do not. We're friends having fun together, having a lot of great sex. But no one's catching feelings."

"You sure about that?" she asked, scooping balls and dropping them in the bucket.

I recalled Liberty's warning to me and how Charlie had said, verbatim, the same thing to her he'd told me. "Positive."

"Mm-hm." She nodded to the other side of the field where Charlie stood with some of the other staff listening to Coach speak. He was looking our way and waved. "If you say so."

A text pings after I park the car along the side of the house. I smile as I read the message.

Charlie: My mother is sending me home with her Tres Leches Cake and instructions for Matt and me not to eat it without you. I may lose a hand, but I'll keep Matt away.

He follows up the text with a picture of him with a pained expression holding a cake with one hand, his other one in his brother's mouth.

Charlie: Come over later? I don't know how long I can hold him back.

I laugh as I type out my reply. *If I survive this day with my parents, I'll be home around seven.*

Charlie: Debuting the pink streaks to the 'rents. Good luck. Remember, it's YOUR hair and it looks stunning on you.

I send back a kissy-face emoji and drop my phone in my bag. With Charlie's encouragement, I took the plunge and dyed hot pink streaks in my hair. Everyone loves it, especially me. But I brace myself for what my mother will say.

I don't have to wait long to find out. She's lying by the pool when I enter the backyard, and I walk over to the chaise to kiss her hello.

"My God, Palmer. What did you do to your hair?" She sits up and inspects the colored locks. "It's temporary, right?"

"If you mean, will it eventually grow out? Then sure, it's temporary." I look around. "Where's Dad? I want to give him his gift."

She clicks her tongue. "Honestly, Palmer. I don't know how you expect to find someone respectable. Your father is in the back trying out his new set of putters."

I walk out past the pool to the end of the property, where Dad had a putting green put in near the treeline. "Happy Father's Day, Dad."

He sinks a short shot and smiles at me. "Palmer. Glad you could make it. Come give your old dad a hug."

We embrace and when he pulls back, he squints at me. "Something's different."

I lift a pink strand. "I dyed my hair."

"No," he says, tilting his head. He tucks his new putter under his arm. "I mean, I'm sure that's true. But something else. You look—"

"Tired? Blotchy?" I gesture to the gauzy pale pink sundress I chose for today. "Too pale?"

"Content." He gives me a warm smile and drapes an arm

around me. "Walk me back to the house. I have to change before the Wainwrights arrive."

"Mom didn't mention they were coming," I say.

"We've become good friends. They're good people. That son of theirs is an outstanding young man."

I roll my eyes. "Please don't tell me you're helping Mom fix us up."

"Wouldn't dream of it," he laughs. "That's your mother's domain."

We walk into the kitchen and while he takes out two beers, one for each of us, I extract the Father's Day card from my bag. He slides me a bottle and I hand over the card.

"I got you something. I thought you might want it now."

"Thank you, sweetheart," he says, opening the envelope. He pulls out the card and opens it, removing the paper inside. "What's this?"

"A private reservation at The Barn," I say. "I heard Mom say you were having trouble getting a reservation anytime soon."

"How did you manage this?" he asks.

I tip the bottle to my lips and take a sip. "I have connections."

My connection being Charlie, of course, who called Miss Annabelle on my behalf and was able to secure a reservation for four next Friday night at the Chef's Table. My parents and their guests, probably the Wainwrights, will have a front-row view of everything happening in the kitchen, plus access to a special menu.

He hugs me and plants a smacking kiss on my cheek. "This is wonderful. Your mother will flip."

"Jeff, Palmer!" my mother calls from the back. "The Wain-wrights are here."

I take Dad's beer for him while he grabs a tray from the

refrigerator with steaks and vegetable kabobs to be cooked. We head outside to greet the guests. I haven't spoken to or seen Boone since the dinner party, but it's like we're old friends. I exchange a quick hug with him and accept cheek kisses from his parents. It's weird to see my parents interact with the Wainwrights. Patsy and Ned are just as well-off as we are, but so much more down-to-earth. It's rubbing off on my parents.

"Ned, want to help me with the grill?" My dad pats his friend on the back and the two of them get busy putting the steaks on.

"Elaine, you have to see the sketches the interior designer came up with for the new houses," Patsy says, joining my mother at the table under the umbrella.

"Can I get you a beer?" I ask Boone.

"Sure." I lead him into the kitchen and open a cold bottle from the fridge. "It's an IPA, hope that's all right. My dad loves the local brewers and it's pretty much all he drinks during the summer."

"This is fine." He takes a sip and leans against the breakfast bar. "So, how have you been? Your season is going well. What are you, 7 and 1 now?"

"I'm impressed you're keeping up," I say. "8 and 1, now. We won our last road game."

He clinks the neck of my bottle with his. "Kudos."

"I think the kids say 'bet' now," I say with a chuckle.

"I'm thirty-four, so I don't think I can be confused for being a kid," Boone says.

I put my bottle down. "Shut up. I didn't think you were more than twenty-five, twenty-six."

He shrugs. "I have a baby face."

"Huh." I take a seat. "So what have you been up to, Boone?"

"Oh, up to my armpits in blueprints, permits, and design details. We've changed the scope of the project somewhat."

"How so?"

Boone sets his beer down and takes his phone out. "Here's an artist rendering of the planned community. See here," he points to a drawing of a maze of interconnected streets lined by large, McMansion-style properties, "this is the original vision. A gated, exclusive community. Fewer houses, but with larger footprints. Starting in the high six-figures to low-seven."

I whistle. "Fancy."

He scrolls to a different rendering. This one shows the same network of streets, but with more houses occupying smaller individual footprints. "After doing some research into the area and talking to my father and the other investors, I've convinced them the smarter approach would be a planned mixed-income community. There will still be a few larger homes with bigger yards for sale, but most of the single-family homes will occupy about a quarter-acre of land and be afford-able for those making around the median wage in the county. We won't earn as much profit right out of the gate, but we will qualify for some state grants to lower construction expenses. Plus, it's the right thing to do. The last thing this county needs is more housing only people working in DC can afford."

He turns off his phone and puts it away with a self-depre-cating laugh. "Sorry. I'm boring you. This cannot be interesting to you in the least."

I put my hand on his arm. "I know a lot of people who had to move further north and west and commute into Frederick for jobs. It will mean so much for people to be able to actually live where they work."

"That's the plan. So when is your next home game?"

"We have two this week. Thursday and again on Saturday."

"Your season must be almost over. Don't the playoffs begin in July?"

"We have about six more regular-season games," I confirm.

"Once we break ground, I won't have a whole lot of time," he says. "Think I can come watch you play this week?"

"I'd love it. Want me to leave you tickets? Thursday or Saturday, or both?"

"How about Thursday?"

My smile wavers a bit at the familiar bite of hurt, but I cover it with an even bigger grin. "Absolutely. I can't wait."

TWENTY-ONE

palmer

I CAN'T REMEMBER the last time I willingly stayed at my parents' later than planned. But the barbecue was a blast, and I attribute it all to the Wainwrights. After enjoying steaks and veggie kabobs on the grill, the six of us played several spirited rounds of cards. Helen, who'd spent the day with her son, returned in time to serve the cheesecake she'd baked earlier in the day and joined us on the patio with a fresh bottle of wine for her, my mother, and Patsy, while my father, Ned, and Boone drank more of my dad's craft beer and debated the virtues of European imports over other varieties. I stuck to Clearly Canadian, since eventually I'd have to drive back home. Practice was too early in the morning to consider staying over; I'd have to leave at the asscrack of dawn to make it in time, and even then, the heavy traffic flowing toward Baltimore from Frederick is too unpredictable. I ended up shooting off a quick text to Charlie apologizing for not being able to make it, and stayed until the Wainwrights left, not getting back to my apartment until close to midnight.

Now, my ass is dragging. I finish strength and conditioning and move to speed and agility drills, sucking wind like a

French Bulldog running uphill in a windstorm. The rest of the day improves little, and I'm grateful when Coach Donovan blows his whistle. I drag myself to the showers and stand under the hot stream until the sound of my teammates fades away.

By the time I towel off and re-enter the locker room, everyone is gone except Tisha. She's rolling up the resistance bands she uses as part of her physical therapy exercises. I dress quickly in my sports bra, running shorts, and oversized sleeveless tee.

"You looked like hell out there today."

I stick my tongue out at her and she snickers.

"Maybe if you'd kept your tongue where it belongs last night, you wouldn't be in such pain this morning. Tell Charlie he has to give you a break for early practices."

"I wasn't with Charlie last night," I say, pinning my hair back with a stretchy headband. "I haven't seen him since Denver."

Tisha whips her head toward me. "Did you end your experiment already? I thought you were waiting until the end of the season."

"No, we're still, um, experimenting. Between the game schedule and family stuff, we haven't had a chance to be together." I swipe on some Carmex and smack my lips together to spread it. "Honestly, though, I think we needed this break. It's been... intense... since we started sleeping together." I lower my voice so only she can hear me, even though it seems like we're alone.

"But that's what you wanted, right?" she says. "Practice at separating feelings from sex."

"I know." I sling my backpack over my shoulder and turn around. "It's just harder than I thought it'd be. I knew going in there wasn't a future with him. I thought it'd just be fun. But sometimes he makes me forget this is pretend. Are you heading home right now, or do you want to go grab a coffee or something?"

"I have to see Diana," she says. "I'd hoped to make it into one more game, but it's not going to happen."

"Damn it, T. I'm sorry."

"Don't be," Tisha says, walking with a more pronounced limp I hadn't noticed before. "You're not the bitch from Tampa who clipped my knee out from under me last season."

"It was a cheap shot."

"She's a cheap bitch." Tisha walked toward the elevators. "Anyway, I need to go upstairs to talk to Diana about next steps and possibilities." Diana Gregson is our General Manager. She took excellent care of all of us, without compromising the team's integrity or success. If there's any chance Tisha can stay with the team post-retirement, Diana would find it.

"Does that mean Wyoming's off the table?" I ask, with possibly too much hope in my voice, judging by the apology in Tisha's reply.

"Nope, still right in the middle of the table. But it's not a done deal, so I need to plan as if it might not happen. Anyway, if you weren't with Charlie setting the sheets on the fire, why are you so drained today?"

We stop by the elevators while I tell her about spending time in Frederick last night and how, for the first time in possibly ever, I enjoyed myself while in the company of my parents. "These people, the Wainwrights, are a good influence on my folks. I don't know how, but they seem to have gotten them to loosen up some. My mother gave me shit about my hair only once. And their son, Boone, is such a sweetheart. He's going to come see our games this week."

"Is he now?" Tisha leans against the wall opposite the elevator doors.

"Don't give me that tone of voice," I huff at her. I punch the up button for her, then turn back around to face her. "We're just friends."

"Does Charlie know about this friend?"

"No, but I don't see why he would care." I don't bother to hide the annoyance creeping into my voice. The elevator arrives with a ding and the doors slide open behind me. "For the umpteenth time, Charlie and I are just having fun. There's nothing there and there never will be. He's a distraction, that's all, a way for me to figure things out."

I turn to hold the door open for Tisha, pulling up short as Liberty steps out of the car. It's clear from her smug grin she overheard at least some of what I was saying to Tisha. My lips thin as I move away from her, and I cast Tisha a wary glance. She returns it with a wide-eyed look of her own. She knows about the last run-in I had with Liberty regarding Charlie.

"Is Coach Arkhady still in her office?" the redhead asks, an innocent smile on her lips. "I came down to speak with her."

"Far as I know," Tisha says, pointing her thumb over her shoulder. Saw the light on when we walked past."

"Thanks." Liberty beams at Tisha, then at me. "You ladies have a lovely day."

"Yeah, you, too," I mutter.

Tisha walks onto the car and shakes her head at me. "She looks like she can't wait to tattle on you. Guess it's a good thing there's nothing real going on between you and Charlie, after all."

charlie

AFTER SPENDING MOST of the past thirty days together, not seeing Palmer for the past five has almost killed me. I can't wait anymore, so I slice up the Tres Leches Cake and take two over to Palmer's at the end of the day. I send her a text I'm on the way, but it doesn't occur to me she might not want me to come over. So I'm not aware of her message begging off until I've already knocked on her door and she answers it with a confused expression on her face. She wears a pair of baggy flannel pants and a sports bra, her hair a staticky mess and dark shadows under her eyes. She looks as beautiful as ever, even bedraggled and exhausted.

"Charlie, what are you doing here?"

"I texted you I was bringing cake over," I say, lifting the plastic container to show her.

"Yeah, I know. And I texted you back that I wasn't feeling up for cake right now. It was a rough practice, and I just want to get to bed early tonight."

My face falls. "Shit, I'm sorry. I didn't check to see if you replied."

I thrust the container out to her. "Here, take it. My mother will have my head if she finds out I never gave any to you. You can have it later as a snack or tomorrow morning for breakfast. I'll let you go back to bed."

She takes the cake and sighs. "Charlie–"

"Hey, no. It's okay." I kiss her forehead. "I overstepped and now I'm going to fix it by leaving. Grab some rest and we'll hook up tomorrow."

"I'm sor–"

"No, don't worry about it." I flash her a smile to show her I'm not disappointed, even though I am. But my feelings aren't what matter right now. "Tomorrow. I'll call you. Okay?"

She nods and I walk away. The door clicks shut behind me and I ride the elevator back to the garage.

The next day, I'm on edge at work. It's now the sixth day of not being with Palmer, and the withdrawal symptoms are starting. I can't focus on the work at hand and end up cutting and re-cutting the same thirty-second Reel fifteen times. All I picture is Palmer, looking like a beautiful wreck last night. She said she'd had a rough practice, but when I look in on the field today, everything is going well. I wait for a break when she can remove her helmet so I can see for myself she's feeling better, and when it finally happens, when I can put eyes on her flushed but smiling face, I return to the office.

Around noon, I receive a text from Palmer.

PALMER

Hey, I'm sorry about last night.

ME

No, I'm sorry for just showing up. Hope you were able to get some rest

PALMER

I did. I'm feeling a lot better. And thank your mom for the cake. It was a delicious breakfast this morning.

ME

LOL Told you

ME

Do you want to get together tonight? I wanna hear how your parents reacted to your new look

PALMER

Dad didn't say anything. Mom sure did, but she restrained herself to only one snide comment.

ME

Sounds like progress. Dinner and a movie later?

PALMER

I have another idea... pick me up at 6!

ME

6 it is

The rest of my day gets better, until Liberty corners me in the break room. She sidles up beside me as I wait for my coffee to brew. She flips her hair over her shoulder and peeks around, as if to ensure we're alone. No one is in the room with us, but the walls are glass, and anyone can see inside, which is the only reason I feel relatively safe in her presence.

"Are you still seeing Palmer?" she asks without preamble.

I run a hand through my hair and sigh. "I'm tired of this, Liberty. I can't keep having the same argument with you. My personal life is none of your business. Period. Full stop. If you don't stop harassing me about it, I'm going to have no choice but to go to Kathryn."

Her mouth gapes open. "Are you seriously threatening me with HR, Charlie? Fine." She lifts her hands in a flourish and lets them drop dramatically before turning to leave. I haven't gotten my sigh of relief out, though, before she spins back around and marches right up to me, her head tilted all the way back to look at me.

"I saw you at the bar the other night. I heard you. I see the way you look at her, talk to her, touch her. I won't pretend to understand why her and not," she inhales a sharp breath, a glassy sheen to her eyes, "not me. I act like a jealous bitch because I am one."

Her watery laugh is without humor. "You really care about her, don't you? It's different for you this time?"

I flex my jaw and look away before nodding slowly. Liberty harrumphs.

"How ironic, then," she says. "Because I overheard her talking to Tisha yesterday. I was downstairs looking for Coach Arkhady, and Palmer didn't realize I was behind her. She was emphatic about how you're only having fun, that you're just a distraction while she figures things out."

I scowl at her. "You're making shit up to stir the pot."

"I'm not," she says calmly. "It's what I heard. I'm telling you because a part of me does care about you, but another, maybe bigger part, is taking pleasure in watching you learn how it feels to be on that side of the equation."

She stalks out of the breakroom. Liberty is trouble and I won't put it past her to make shit up. But what she said has a ring of truth to it. A fun distraction. A plan to break old patterns. That's how this began with Palmer, at least for her. It's always been about more for me, and I thought I was making progress. If what Liberty said she overheard is true, then have I just been spinning my wheels this whole time?

I close my eyes and conjure up the memory of Palmer the first night we made love, the wonder in her eyes, the heat, the connection. I didn't imagine it. I know I didn't.

I add cream to my coffee and return to my desk, eager to

finish up and resolved to remind myself–and Palmer–what we have is more than a distraction as far as I'm concerned.

It's a little after six when I knock on Palmer's door. She swings it open, a hand resting on her hip, and her small purse slung across her body. A pair of sunglasses holds the hair off her face, and she's wearing cut-off shorts with a deep purple sleeveless top that highlights the definition and tone of her arms. I admire the smooth muscles with my eyes, my groin already tightening in anticipation of touching them later.

Whoa, boy. Don't get ahead of yourself.

"You're late," she chides, but there's no heat in her voice.

"Long day at the office," I sigh and look down at my navy blue trousers and silvery-gray Van Heusen button-down. "I haven't changed yet, and I'm greatly overdressed."

She reaches up to undo a couple more buttons, exposing more of the dark hair covering my pecs. She pats my chest. "There. Now, come on. We're going to be late."

"Where are we going?"

"You'll see."

She takes my hand and we ride the elevator to street level. Wherever we're going, it's within walking distance. While we walk, she tells me about the party at her parents' house and her mother's muted reaction to her hair.

"I had a really good time, which seems so odd to say." She shakes her head. "I never have a good time at home. It's why I jumped at moving in with Brennan at the time. I had to move away."

I swing her hand to my lips and plant a kiss on her knuckles. "I'm glad things are getting better between you."

"I'm hopeful they may come to the game on Saturday. I'm leaving tickets at Will Call just in case."

We turn a corner and she announces, "Here we are."

We're at a storefront with a large bay window, Charm City Inkslingers scrolled in on the glass in a retro font. Inside, a guy sits in a chair with his arm outstretched while another man in leather and wearing a pair of bifocals uses a tattoo gun on his inner forearm.

I turn to her, my brows raised in surprise. "A tattoo shop?"

"Yep." She pulls open the old-fashioned door and drags me inside, the tinkle of a bell announcing our arrival. I'm still not sure if we're here for me or her, as she strides up to the counter still holding onto my hand for dear life.

"Hi. I'm Palmer. I have a six-thirty appointment?"

The woman behind the counter taps on an iPad, her blue hair swinging around her face as she moves. She has a tiny hoop piercing one eyebrow and a metal ring hooked between her nostrils. Her arms are tapestries of intricate Japanese art in bold reds, blacks, and greens.

"You're getting a tat?" I ask. Palmer nods.

"Yes. And you're going to hold my hand through it."

palmer

I PEEL the bandage off my tattoo and admire it in the bedroom mirror. "I can't believe I did it."

"I can." Charlie is stretched across my bed, watching me. "You've got more badass in you than you give yourself credit for."

I look over my shoulder at him. "Not sure I can show my mother, though. Unless I wear something short, she probably won't ever see it. So maybe not that badass."

He sits up and holds open his arms. I walk into them and stand between his knees. He squeezes my backside. "Yes. That badass."

His hands slide into my shorts, and, already unzipped, he pushes them to the floor. He grips my hips and turns me to the side so he can inspect the tat up close. I opted for something small for my first one, a little lacrosse stick against the Battle logo with a daisy accent in stark black linework. It's like a sticker. "Didn't she do a great job?"

He moves over it with a light touch. "It's perfect. But why a daisy and not the state flower to go with the flag?"

"Black-eyed Susans are pretty, but daisies are my

favorite." I gesture to the painting on my wall and the daisy-adorned bedspread. "You haven't noticed?"

He presses a soft kiss over the tat, then turns me facing him and presses a kiss over my panties. "I've only been noticing you," he murmurs against my thighs. "I missed you."

"Me, too." I thread my fingers through his hair and let my head fall back as he blows a stream of hot air over my pussy. His hands grip my backside, holding me upright as if he knows I'm seconds from melting into a puddle at his feet. He nuzzles his nose in between my legs and nips at my inner thigh.

"I need to get inside you," he growls, lapping at my heat through my panties.

"Please," I pant, my pulse already topping out. I hook my hands in the sides of my underwear and slide them down, kicking them and my shorts to the side. Charlie grunts and dives in, holding me still while he laps and licks and sucks at all my sensitive spots.

He grips my hips and turns to toss me on the bed. I scoot upward, stripping off my top and bra, while he undoes his belt and lowers his trousers. He crawls onto the bed over me, fastening his mouth over mine. I work at his buttons and push the shirt off his shoulders. He's more tan, but his hot, sleek skin and rippling muscles are the same, and touching him is like coming home. I sigh into his mouth and suck on his tongue as I spread my legs around his thick thighs. With my heels, I finish pushing his boxers and pants off his legs. We're panting and naked, his cock sliding along my slick folds.

"Charlie, please," I moan, reaching between us to grab his steel. It's been only a days, but it might as well have been a lifetime since he's filled me, and I'm aching for him.

"Hang on, baby," he says, nipping at my ear. "I need a condom."

It takes him seconds to grab one from the box on my nightstand and slide it on. As soon as it's in place, I yank him down on top of me and hook my ankles together at the small of his back so I can push him in. He grunts once he's fully seated, and we start rocking together.

"My baby's greedy tonight," he pants in my ear as he nips my lobe and licks the spot he knows drives me crazy.

"It's been way too long," I moan. "Your dick has spoiled me. My vibrator doesn't do the trick anymore."

"No?" He lifts up on his arms and pivots his hips, each plunge of his thick cock inside of me setting off sparks. "Where is it?"

"What?"

"Your vibrator. Battery-operated boyfriend. Dildo."

"I think," I swallow thickly. "I think it's only a dildo if it doesn't have batteries."

"Yours does."

"And a remote." I arch my back, encouraging him to go deeper. "Why are we talking about this now? You're here. I don't need BOB."

He pulls out of me so fast he give me pussy whiplash. I very nearly cry. "Hey!"

"Just a sec." He digs around in my nightstand drawer and comes up with my vibrating little friend. I blush as he holds it up with an amused expression. "How can I measure up to him?"

It's thick with simulated veins and ridges along the shaft, about nine inches long, and a set of artificial balls that vibrate. It's comparable in girth and length to Charlie. I don't tell him I traded in my original bullet vibrator after we started messing around, because after experiencing Charlie's sex, the little vibrator that could couldn't anymore.

"Charlie," I whine.

"Palmer," he mimics me. He roots around in the drawer

and comes up with the tiny remote. "So, how does this work? Do you put it all inside you and press the big red button? Or do you work your way up to it? Show me."

I lick my lips and reach for it. His eyes track my every move as I rub the toy down my body. I roll the tip around my nipples, watching his eyes go dark. The rubber doesn't glide against my skin easily. Normally I add a bit of lube to help things along, but tonight I open my mouth and suck the toy between my lips, spreading the saliva around with my tongue. A low, feral hum comes out of him, his eyes still captivated by what I'm doing.

I drag the vibrator between my breasts and over my curls, teasing my entrance with the tip. He's still watching my hands, so I whisper to grab his attention. "The remote has three settings. Those two little buttons and the big red one. Don't push the big one yet."

He grunts his assent and flicks one of the buttons with his thumb. The impostor cock begins to vibrate a light rhythm. I work it all around my heat, putting extra pressure against the hooded bud of my sex. He increases the intensity and I moan in pleasure, arching my back and spreading my legs even wider so he can watch me fuck myself. I dip the head of the wand into my channel and circle it around before pulling it out and doing it again. Each time, I move it a little farther. Charlie modulates the speed of the vibration back and forth between slow and medium, a wild grin on his face as he watches every little movement. I start sliding the toy faster and deeper between my folds, planting my heels on the bed to give me better purchase while I lift my hips and change the angle. My eyes flutter close, the undulating vibrations teasing my nerves and bringing me to the edge. With the hand not holding the vibrator, I circle my clit with my fingers, fucking myself two ways as I chase my release. Faster, harder. When I'm at my peak, I shout at him to hit the red button. The rubber balls attached to the toy vibrate with a frenzy. I hold the shaft inside me as the vibrations shake loose my orgasm. My fingers fly over my clit until I break with a scream of ecstasy.

Before I even begin to come down, the toy is pulled out of me and Charlie is on top, levering himself into me, stringing out my bliss until we're both cursing and chanting, our breaths mingling, our arousal heavy in the air. He drags out a final roar from his chest as I shiver beneath him, my throat raw.

We lay entwined for so long, I'm not confident either of us will ever be able to leave this bed. When I say as much to Charlie, he laughs. "I'm good with that, Coco. I'd give up my whole life to lie here and watch you pleasure yourself. As long as I get to play, too."

Me, too. I could stay here forever in his arms. But I keep that little tidbit to myself.

TWENTY-FOUR

charlie

I'M STILL RIDING the high from the other night with Palmer. Every night spent with her is increasingly hot. When she put the whole toy in her mouth, I could've come right then. But I'm glad I waited because it just got better and better. I noted the D-cell batteries it took and added them to my shopping list. I will never let my girl be without her power.

Unfortunately, we haven't had a chance to speak much since. Tonight's a crucial game. With only a handful of games left, including tonight's against our Boston, there's no room for error if we want to make it into the playoffs. Only one other team has a better record than ours, but that can change in a heartbeat with a loss. Everyone from the coaches and players to the front office staff has been on edge, making sure everything goes exactly right. I've sent Palmer some texts of encouragement, but otherwise I've stayed out of the way. She doesn't need any distractions.

Tonight, I station myself in the VIP 200 Suite, box seats on the 200-level reserved for players' guests, which provides the best vantage point of the bench area. It also has the added benefit of giving me the best view of Palmer in goal when she's on this side of the field. We take the first draw and put points on the board in just under forty-two seconds, setting the tone for the entire game.

Once a quarter, I walk around to check on things, but mostly I stay in one place. The interns, Emma and Benji, are out in the crowd, capturing content for us to put up on the socials. Two other members of our department are on the sidelines, getting all the on-field action. The footage I get of the players on the bench will be used in behind-the-scenes multimedia at some point. It's not the most important, so I have the chance to enjoy the game.

One of the other guys in the box with me is also enjoying the game , and my goalie in particular. He cheers with his whole chest whenever Palmer stops a ball. "All right, York! Wooo!"

I try to figure out who he's with, what player he's here to see, and the only conclusion I can come to is he's here for Palmer. She's the only one he's specifically cheering for. At halftime, I'm about to introduce myself, but a call comes over the walkie from Emma, who needs help staging the halftime games for the fans.

The game ends in a crushing defeat for Boston. Palmer strips off her helmet and celebrates with her team. Even from here, I can see she's red-faced, sweat-soaked hair stuck to her forehead, but it's the pure joy radiating off her that makes her the loveliest person down there. I pack up my equipment and jog down to the tunnels to meet her, but Dante intercepts me. I'll have to catch her on the way home.

Forty-five minutes later, I've finished and put my equipment away and I ride down to the ground floor to try to catch Palmer on her way out. The night vibrates with excitement, and the lower level of the stadium buzzes with celebration as I step off the elevator. Someone is belting out Miley Cyrus, and I'd bet my paycheck it's Marisol. I walk down the hall to the tunnel exit to the parking lot, where a gaggle of friends and family wait for their players. I say hello to a few I recognize, then pull up short at the sight of the same guy from the suite.

He leans against the wall, tapping on his phone. A few inches shorter than me, he's in dark jeans and a Chesapeake Red Hawks shirt, his dirty blond hair combed and gelled into a tidy coif. The Bulova on his wrist and Versace trainers speak of his wealth. Maybe he senses me staring at him, because he looks up, giving me a friendly smile. There's nothing inherently wrong with the guy, so I can't explain the sudden urge to punch his bland face.

"How's it going?" he asks.

"Good." I fold my arms. "Who are you waiting for?"

Before he answers, the door to the inner part of the stadium, where the locker rooms, training areas, and coaches' offices are, bursts open and a stream of chattering women flows through. I congratulation them on their way out, giving and receiving a few fist bumps. Then I see her. Palmer steps through, freshly showered, eyes as bright as a sunny day in Fiji. Her mouth is a ripe strawberry, pink lips plump and juicy. I gravitate toward her but stop, feet turning to clay as she turns to the other guy and greets him with a hug. I can't look away, the noise around me becoming a discordant din. They're smiling and talking, but I can't tell what they're saying.

The guy points a thumb toward the exit, and she nods her head. I force myself to move, to intercept them before they leave. I need to know who the fuck this guy is and why Palmer is leaving with him. I'd assumed we would be cele-brating tonight. Together. Alone.

"Palmer," I call out. She stops and faces me, lighting up for a moment before her smile falters. I paste a toothy grin on my face and lean in to wrap my arms around her. I kiss her temple. "Great game out there. You killed it."

I release her from the embrace, but leave one arm draped across her shoulders. I reach out my hand to the other guy. "Charlie Salinas."

The man shakes it, a smile as fake as mine gracing his features. "Boone Wainwright."

I cast Palmer a questioning look. She'd mentioned the Wainwrights as the older couple her parents had befriended, but this guy didn't look like a friend of her father's. She picks up on my silent question.

"Boone is the son of my parents' friends," she explains. "He wanted to come to a game, so I set aside tickets and a pass for him."

"What a hell of a game to come to," he adds, his smile growing genuine as he talks to Palmer. "You almost shut them out. The two that got by took weird bounces, so I wouldn't even consider those anything you did wrong."

Palmer laughs and subtly steps forward. I let my arm drop. "Yeah, you drill and drill, but sometimes you can't help the bounce."

"I made reservations if you're still up for a later din-ner," Boone says. He glances at me and puts on the fake smile again. "Maybe your friend here would like to join us?"

I open my mouth to accept, but then Liberty's words come back to me. *I'm fun. A distraction.* My whole purpose exists to help Palmer reset her love life, teach her how not to fall in love first by teaching her how not to fall at all. I'm suddenly nause-ated, overheating. I step backward and wave my hand. "No, you guys go ahead. I've got other plans. Just came to congratulate our star goalie here."

I flash her a smile and ignore her look of—of what? Jealousy? Confusion? No, those are what I'm probably broadcasting right now. "I'll see you on the field."

"Charlie," she says. But I've already turned around.

charlie

"WHY ARE YOU SO MOPEY?" My brother throws his wadded-up pair of socks at my head.

I bat them away and flip him off. "I'm not mopey. Tired. It was a long day."

"Where's Palmer tonight?" Matt flops down on the other end of the sectional and puts his bare feet up on the table. "I haven't seen her around lately and you've been home more often than not."

"We don't spend every waking moment together," I snap, smashing the buttons on the remote as I try to find something to watch. "Not like we're a real couple."

"Ah." Matt sets his bottle of beer down on the table next to him. "So that's the problem. Still haven't convinced her to make this thing between you permanent?"

I settle on the Orioles game in its eighth inning and toss the remote on the coffee table. "I don't want to talk about it."

"All right." Matt reclaims his beer and takes a long pull. I can't focus on the game, and I can't stop checking my phone for a message I suspect isn't coming. I've all but been blatantly ignoring her since she went out with that guy Boone last week, so it serves me right her own texts to me have dropped off. I tell myself it's a cooling-off period, but what I'm really doing is licking my wounds.

"I was supposed to have the season," I finally say. My head rests on my fist against the arm of the couch, and I stare at the TV while I talk.

"Last week, she invited a friend of the family to the game and then went on a date with him."

"You sure it was a date?" Matt asks. "You just said it's a friend of the family."

"It was a fucking date," I growl. "You should see the way he was looking at her during the game, and the way–"

I tighten my lips. "Forget it."

Matt sits up and snags the remote, muting the volume of the game. "The way what, *Carlito*?"

I grind my molars and force the words out. "The way she looked at him. Liberty was right."

"Whoa, back up," Matt says, leaning on his knees. "Liberty from the office? The one who hates you? What could she possibly be right about?"

I tell him about my conversation with Liberty in the breakroom and what she claimed to overhear. "I didn't believe it was meant the way she took it. But this guy last night is exactly the type she dates. The kind she wants to settle down with. He's rich, clean-cut, probably some kind of hedge fund manager or lawyer. His parents are good friends with hers. He's exactly what they want for her."

"Who cares? Isn't what she wants the thing that matters?"

I run a hand through my hair. "She wants their approval. With this guy, she'll get it."

"You don't think they'd approve of you?"

I side-eye him. "I don't think I fit the image they have in mind for their only daughter."

Matt sits back and picks up his beer. "So what are you going to do? You callin' it?"

A chasm rips open in my chest. "I don't want a repeat of what happened with Angela. Not that I think she'd cheat on me. But I also don't want to keep waiting for her to wake up one day and decide she's done with this little experiment. I'm too old to keep putting myself out there."

"When have you put yourself on the line since Angela? Palmer is the first and only woman I've seen you take a risk on in years."

I spread my arms out. "And look how that's going."

"Stop being a coward." Matt's words knock me back and stun me into silence. He slams his bottle down, causing a small geyser of foam to leak onto the table. "You say you didn't make a move on her before because of her boyfriend. But I think you were afraid."

He shifts to the edge of the cushion and lays into me hard. "You put her on a pedestal, and as long as she was taken, you had an excuse that let you avoid the risk of rejection. Meanwhile, you fuck around like your dick's about to fall off the second you stop using it, but it's okay because you're upfront about sharing your dick and not your life. That's in reserve for your untouchable crush. Now, you finally have a chance with the woman you've had heart eyes for, and what will you do at the first sign of conflict? You're gonna cut and run, and use the excuse you're only protecting yourself from getting hurt again, because you're too chickenshit to fight for what you want. She'll go back on the pedestal, this time as the one who got away, and she'll become what Angela has been for the past decade—your excuse not to risk loving someone."

He sits back and takes a long pull of beer. The silence between stretches out for several long minutes as I try to figure out what do with my ass that was just handed to me. I absorb the lashing, realizing he is one hundred percent right, and scrub a hand down my face. "I'm a fucking *pendejo*."

"No. You're just acting like one." Matt sighs and gentles his voice. "Look, I don't want to see you with another broken heart, either. But this sleeping around is getting old, and I think you know it. You wanted Palmer to give you a chance. You need to give her one, too. If you really believe she's it for you, then you gotta man up and stop playing these games. You know Mama keeps hinting about *los nietos*."

"You're the oldest," I remind him with a snort. "Why don't you get right on that while I figure this out first?"

"I'm working on it," Matt says, his lips twitching. "Gotta convince Bianca to marry me first, then we can move on to making grandkids."

I sit up and nearly spill my own drink. "For real? You're thinking of proposing? How did I not know this?"

"You haven't asked."

"Damn. Congratulations."

Matt grunts. "Don't jinx it."

"Oh, come on. She's gonna say yes. For whatever weird reason, that woman's nuts over you."

A reluctant smile curves his lips. "Pretty crazy about her, too."

An unexpected pang of envy spears through me. My brother has been quietly preparing a new ilfe with the woman of his dreams while I've been out screwing around, pining for my own dream girl. Now I have her and I'm letting old insecurities get in the way of keeping her. My brother is right. I've been acting like a cowardly asshole.

"All right, *Carlito*," my brother says, taking a tissue and wiping up the little spill. "Are we done talking about our feelings? Because it's the bottom of the ninth and the O's are one out away from beating the Yankees."

We settle back to watch the rest of the game, which goes into two overtime innings. But by the time the Orioles squeak out a win, I've already figured out what I'm going to do about Palmer. Starting with an apology.

TWENTY-SIX

BOONE and I had a lovely dinner after our win against Boston last week, but I couldn't keep my mind off Charlie or the weird way we'd parted. After dessert and distracted conversation on my part, which I waved off as exhaustion, Boone dropped me off at the apartment. I hadn't heard from Charlie all evening and debated whether I should reach out. In the end, I went to bed and had a restless sleep, figuring I'd deal with it in the morning.

But then I didn't hear much from him over the next few days, and I didn't see him at all after Saturday's game. On Sunday, he had supper with his family in Annapolis, while travel and practice kept us apart for several days after. His messages to me were—okay, I guess. They lacked a lot of the flirtatious intensity I'd come to enjoy. I could feel him pulling away and chalked it up to the end of the season coming.

This is all part of the lesson for me. I won't become clingy or try to orchestrate ways to keep him, as I would've in the past. If it's ending, it's ending. I'll simply walk away with fond memories and a locked-down heart, exactly my goal when I started all this with Charlie. The ache in my chest is nothing to worry about. Probably indigestion from Taco Tuesday.

Practice is intense as we start heading into the playoffs. After another scorching day on the field, I shower and change, checking my phone to find a number of messages from my mother asking me to call her "ASAP!" Boone has also left a message thanking me for the tickets and suggesting dinner next week. I mark that one to reply to later. And Rania has sent me a text asking if we could talk. *Delete*. There's nothing from Charlie, which is no longer a surprise. Was he jealous of Boone? Because it almost seemed that way. I dismiss the notion. Charlie doesn't do jealousy because Charlie doesn't do serious.

My teammates are swarming around someone outside the exit. As I stroll closer, I see it's Charlie. He's holding out a tray of milky white iced drinks. A chorus of "Thanks, Charlie" resounds as they each take a cup. There's one left when I get up to him, though it's a darker shade than the others were.

He plucks it out of the tray and hands it to me with a flourish. "Double mocha salted caramel with oatmilk, no whip, light ice."

I eye him with suspicion, but take the iced latte. "You bought everyone iced lattes?"

"I wanted to buy you an iced latte, your favorite. But I know you don't want to call unnecessary attention to us, so I bought everyone a drink and figured no one would be the wiser."

I cock an eyebrow. "You got everyone double mocha salted caramel lattes?"

He widens his eyes comically. "Heavens, no. They all got vanilla lattes. Seemed the safest choice."

"Definitely the most basic," I joke. "Thanks. I can use the pick-me-up."

"Are you heading home?" he asks, walking me to my car.

"Yeah. Coach whipped us pretty good today."

"So no plans?" He opens my door after I unlock it.

"Other than a pizza, this latte, and some faux Thin Mints I picked up at Aldi, nope. No plans." I toss my bag on the passenger seat and slide behind the wheel.

"Will Boone be joining you?" His voice is even, but his gaze wavers.

"No, he's back in Frederick." I bite my bottom lip. "Charlie—"

"How about I come over?" he says, interrupting me. "I was hoping we could talk some."

My chest tightens. This is it. He's ending it. Despite my mental bravado over the past few days, my shoulders sag as I start the car. "Okay."

"I'll bring the pizza." He shuts the door and taps the top of the car before sauntering away. I squeeze my eyes shut for a second and breathe through my nose, then put the car in gear and head out. I don't want to see him walking away.

The humidity is high today, and even within the covered garage, the air is so thick that stepping out of my car and to the elevator is like sludging through molasses. I take another shower and reapply my moisturizer, then fret in front of the closet. Do I go with comfy as I planned? My ultra-soft Vuori joggers and brushed cotton sleeveless tee would be my first choice. Or do I go the seductive route with a low-cut fitted tank top and running shorts to show off the tattoo? Maybe the vintage swing dress I thrifted last week? It's cute and feminine. I don't want to look like I'm trying too hard. That's what the old me would've done.

The knock on the door forces me to grab the first thing in front of me, which is how I end up wearing a pink zippered terry cloth cover-up. My wet hair hangs like strings around my face, but I can't worry about it now. A glance through the peep-hole confirms it's Charlie, and I swing open the door, greeting him with a smile stretched so wide it hurts my ears. His smile isn't as brilliant and it only shows one dimple, which causes me to dial down the sunshine a few notches. He holds up a pizza box. "Anchovies and extra garlic, right?"

I grin at the inside joke. "Only if topped with pickled jalapenos."

He walks past me to put the pizza on the small bistro table inside the kitchen while I close and bolt the door. "One of these days, you're going to try pickled jalapenos and you'll thank me for it."

"Hah." I join him at the table. "When you try black pudding."

He shudders and pulls a face. I start to relax as I gather our plates. "Haven't seen much of you lately," I say, the lightness in my tone belying my anxiety.

"You know how it is coming up to playoff season," he says, opening the lid to reveal a very normal pepperoni and green peppers. "Coach has been working you guys hard. We're just as busy."

"We've only had the one loss this season, so there's a lot of pressure." I hold the plates while he slides slices for each of us on them.

"Heard Tisha won't be able to play in one final game."

"They wanted to perform surgery now, but she talked them into waiting until the season is over. She's been assisting Donovan with coaching, and I think that might be her next move. She's so good at it. Beer? Wine? Coke?"

"Beer, thanks."

His brows rise as he takes the can of Natty Boh from me. "Since when do you keep Natty on hand?"

I shrug and grab a can of Coke for myself. "Since you told me it's your comfort beer."

I realize as soon as the words are out they were a mistake. Casual flings don't do things like keep a favorite beverage on hand. I try to brush it off. "There was a six-pack at the register when I was picking up the wine."

"I appreciate it." He moves the pizza box to the counter to make room at the table for us to eat, then holds out the chair for me.

"So what else have you been up to?" I ask, dabbing the excess grease off the slice with a napkin. "How's Matt?"

"He's good. Actually, he's engaged." Charlie cracks open the can.

"Congratulations. That's exciting."

He takes a sip. "Bianca wants a Christmas wedding, so when I'm not at work, I've been helping with wedding preparations."

"Oh." I take a bite of pizza. "That explains why I haven't heard from you much."

"Yeah," he says, putting his slice down. "About that."

I hold up a hand, the pizza turning to dust in my stomach. "It's okay, Charlie. You don't have to say it. This arrangement we have had a deadline, and now things are getting busy, so you want to end it early. It's okay. I get it."

Charlie drops his slice. "That's not what I'm saying at all. In fact, I thought you might be finished with me."

My brow creases. "So you aren't ending our fling?"

He releases a quiet laugh. "No. No, I'm not."

He opens his mouth like he wants to say more, then closes it again and picks up his pizza. I hum as relief flows through my veins.

"Can I ask why you thought I was ending things?" I stare at him in puzzlement.

He plays with his can and doesn't look at me when he answers. "Thought you might have met someone, someone you thought you could have a real relationship with."

"Boone?" A fuzzy feeling warms me from the inside. He *is* jealous. "We're only friends. I'm not ready for anything more. I mean, that's the whole point of our fling here, right?"

"Right," he says, pressing his lips together. He sets the already empty can down.

"Do you want another?" I ask, pointing at the can.

He stands and holds his hand out to me. "What I want is you. Now that we've cleared things up, how 'bout we make up for lost time?"

TWENTY-SEVEN

palmer

I'M glad I went with the simple terry coverup, because it only takes him a few minutes to divest me of it on the way down the hall. We enter my bedroom and I push him down on the edge of the bed, straddling him as I yank off his shirt. I hold his face while I plunge my tongue between his lips, his hungry kisses matching mine in intensity. His growing bulge is evident between my legs, and I rock back and forth, seeking pleasure from the friction against my silk panties.

"Uhn-uhn," he murmurs in my mouth. He stands, lifting me at the same time. It's such a turn-on to be with a man who can manhandle me like I'm a delicate doll instead of a lumbering giant. He drops me on the bed and makes quick work of his shorts and briefs. I prop myself up on my elbows and watch his cock spring into action, squeezing my thighs together against a small rush of wetness.

He grunts and crawls over me. "How expensive were these panties?"

"They were 5 for $25 at Victoria's Secret."

With a hard tug, he rips them off my body, and I gasp when

he pushes my legs apart. "Fuck, I missed your perfect little cunt, always so wet and waiting for me."

"I missed your dirty, filthy mouth," I pant.

He waggles his brows, settling himself in my valley. With his thumbs, he spreads my swollen lips and spears me with his tongue. I pull on his hair, pressing him into me, crying out as he flicks my bud with the tip of his tongue, then clamps his mouth over me. He sucks, hard, and I come off the bed with a shriek. The sensation is intense. I can't rein it in, can't control my body's spasms, can't stop chanting "Yesyesyesyesyes" while I come on his tongue, his lips, the fingers he slips inside me.

But I'm not finished. I'm riding a wave that's rising up and over, and I want more, need more, before I crash down. "I need you inside of me, Charlie. Right. Fucking. Now."

He starts to lean over toward the nightstand where the condoms are, but I can't wait. I don't want to wait. "Charlie, now."

"Let me protect you, love."

"I'm clean," I say. "And I have an IUD."

He stares down at me, his eyes dark and unfathomable, lips glistening with my honey. In a voice like smoked bourbon, he says, "I've never, not ever, gone bare before."

My breaths continue to heave out of me. I push aside the tingle of disappointment. It's a reckless proposition, anyway. I'm just so hot and so horny and I want to feel every inch of him when he pushes into me, feel him filling me so completely. I bite my lip and squirm beneath him.

He searches my face, dragging his gaze down my body and then back. "Are you sure? I get tested regularly, and I'm also clear.

My lungs seize. "I'm sure if you are," I say, my voice cracked and husky.

"Fuck, Palmer," he grinds out. He hitches my legs higher on his hips and bends. His bellend presses against me as he slants his mouth over mine and kisses the last of my breath out of me. He inches inside me. Every ridge draws against my walls, stoking the flames as he slides his way inside slowly. He seats himself all the way, balls resting against my ass.

"I want to savor every fucking second of this," he says. "I want to live right here, like this, for the rest of my life."

His eyes close and I'm fascinated by the fierce concentration. I'm also restless with the need to move. I circle my hips, eliciting a hiss from him. His eyes fly open and he stares at me in wonder.

"Please," I plead.

His jaw tightens as he withdraws all the way to the tip before slamming back into me. His heavy balls slap aganst my ass and I cry out, stars dancing in my vision. "Again," I beg.

He pulls out and thrusts back in a hard, punishing rhythm, rocking the headboard into the wall. It hurts, but hurts so good, and I don't ever want him to stop fucking me like this. Maybe I say it out loud, but I have no control over the sounds coming out of my mouth and I have no idea if I'm even forming words. Each thrust forces them out from the depths of my soul. His animalistic grunts turn me on, and in no time, I'm a quivering, shivering mess around him as my second orgasm rocks through me.

"Fuck, I can't hold back," he growls.

"Then don't," I strain, riding the aftershocks of my bliss. "Fill me, Charlie. Take me how you want me."

He pulls all the way out, but before I can protest, he flips me over and yanks me to my knees by my hips. It's rough and feral, and I tilt my hips to give him as much access as he needs. He splits me and the angle of his cock is putting pressure near where I need it. I start the climb again, my third release so close, so close, so close, a hair's breadth away. I rub my clit, trying to find the right combination to set me off again. He throbs inside me, my channel squeezing him, and he shudders like he's a moment away from falling off the edge. I want to be there with him when he goes, or at least close behind.

"This feels so good. You feel so good, so fucking good." he wheezes. "Are you ready, baby?"

"Almostalmostalmost," I chant. I'm on the edge furiously working my clit, seconds away from happily dying. "Don't hold back. I'll be right behind you."

"Fuck that," he roars. "You're coming with me."

He thrusts deep with a few more pumps, and I'm suddenly soaring. His shouts blend with mine as we both vibrate, his hot fluid spurting into me. We fall, together, and tumble in a heap on the mattress, breathless, sticky, and spent.

He rolls off me, sucking in air. I turn onto my back, my chest still heaving. I stare at the ceiling, waiting for my soul to come back to me. He grasps my hand and brings it to his mouth.

"Amazing," he coos.

"Yeah." It's all I can squeak out in between gasps.

We lay together in silence until our breaths are controlled and our pulses slow from an all-out sprint to a lazy jog. He turns on his side and props himself up on his elbow, tracing lazy circles around my stomach. "Why?"

"Why what?" I ask, stifling a yawn.

"Why did you want to skip the protection? Weren't you worried with my, er, experience, I wouldn't be a safe partner?"

I turn my head to look at him. "No. I know if you didn't think you could keep me safe, you would've said so. As to why I asked... I don't know. In the heat of the moment, it felt right."

"And now? The heat has cooled, do you still think it was the right thing?"

I put a hand to his cheek. "I don't regret it, if that's what you're asking. And if you're game, I'm all for tossing out the latex for as long as we're doing this with only one another."

"Me neither." A tiny crease forms above the bridge of his nose. "But if we do this, we're not fucking other people."

"Of course not."

"Or going to dinner with them," he adds with a scowl. I feather a kiss over his lips.

"Okay. It's only you, Charlie."

He gives me his two-dimple smile. "And it's only you, Palmer."

charlie

WE FALL asleep in each other's arms. I can't think of a time when I was more satisfied, or more humbled. That she trusts me with her body means the world. We've taken a big step forward, and when we wake at her alarm in the morning, there's a lightness in my heart I never knew could exist.

Only it turns out it's not her alarm. Her phone is ringing the Star Wars Imperial March on repeat. With a shout of frustration, she untangles herself from me and half-climbs, half-falls out of bed. On the way out of the bedroom, she kicks the hassock at the foot of the bed. "Son of a BITCH!"

She hops on one foot while she reaches for the robe hanging off a hook on her door. I pat the space she'd just occupied. "Come back to bed and I'll kiss it all better."

"I can't, I have to find my stupid phone." The music stops, but then it starts up again. She listens for a beat before rushing out the door. "Hello?"

She speaks from the other room in low murmurs. I check the clock—six am. Who the hell is calling at six am on a Saturday?

Her voice rises. I'm alert now, her distress finishing the job of waking me that her phone started. I throw on my briefs and walk out to find her pacing the living room.

"*Mother*," she snaps into the phone. "You're being unreasonable... yeah, you are... Playoffs start this week. I won't have time—"

I make my way to the kitchen to start the coffee while she listens to her mother on the other end of the line. I sneak glances at her as I measure out the water and grounds, set the filter in the basket, and start it brewing. I can't hear what is being said to her, but she started the conversation full of fire. Now, it seems her flame is being doused with every passing moment. Finally, she ends the call and drops onto the couch, slump-shouldered and defeated.

I find milk and hazelnut creamer in the fridge and pour us each a mug, adding a splash of milk to mine and a heavy dollop of creamer to hers. I set her mug in front of her and lean against the doorway, blowing on mine before taking a sip. "Want to talk about it?"

She pulls her knees to her chest and wraps her arms around them. "It was my mother."

"I gathered. What's so urgent she had to call and upset you before the sun has barely cleared the horizon?"

"She gets up at five, so this isn't early to her. I've been ducking her calls the past few days, just because, so I figured I'd better answer and see what she wants."

I sip my coffee, the hot liquid burning the tip of my tongue. "And?" I prompt when she doesn't continue.

"I told you my ex is marrying my cousin." She wipes a finger across her eyelid. "My mother is hosting an engagement lunch for them tomorrow and she wants me to be there."

Rage kindles and burns inside, at her ex, at her cousin, but mostly at her mother. "First of all, why there, and secondly, why do you have to go?"

She gives a watery laugh. "My Aunt Dory and Uncle Frank are in the process of renovating their house, and I guess the bride-to-be didn't want to have it at a restaurant. She wanted something more private—for all fifty guests."

I put my mug down and sit next to her, enfolding her into my arms. She leans her head against my chest and sniffles, wiping her nose with the sleeve of her robe. "Don't think I'm crying because I miss Brennan."

"Okay." I smooth down her hair.

"Or think I'm jealous. They deserve each other, and I honestly don't care if they get married."

"I don't," I soothe.

"I'm just so angry." She sits up and rubs her face with her robe. I look around and spot a box of tissues on the end table and hand it to her.

"Thanks," she says, using the tissues to dry her eyes.

"It's understandable you're angry, Coco. What they did is seriously fucked up."

She balls up the tissue and tosses it on the table. "No, not angry at them. Angry at my mom. I understand Rania is her niece, but I'm her daughter. Why the hell does she think it's okay to host an engagement party for my ex-boyfriend and my *cousin*? And to demand my presence on top of it."

My irritation spikes. If I didn't think it'd make Palmer's life harder, I'd call her mother back and give the woman a reality check. "You're an adult, Palmer. She can't demand your presence at anything."

"Sounds good, in theory. But my parents are all I have. I don't have brothers or sisters, or a big extended family like yours. I have to go. But I'm so mad she's putting me in this position to look like a fool. A total loser."

"Hey, now. Not possible." I grasp her chin and turn her face to mine. Her usually lively eyes are dull with sadness. "You are not a fool or a loser. Haven't we been over this before?"

She offers me a weak smile and brushes a quick kiss to my lips. Her phone begins playing a lyrical melody. She swipes it off. "Time for practice."

I stand. "I promised Bianca I'd take Matt shopping for wedding suits. She doesn't trust his taste. Which is fair; left to his own devices, we'd probably all be wearing carpenter jeans and flannels."

This gets a chuckle out of her. "All right. See you later?"

"You bet." kiss her then smack her ass. "Now let's get out of here before Coach has you doing wind sprints for being late."

TWENTY-NINE
charlie

LATER, I text Palmer about meeting Bianca, Matt, and me for dinner. She can't because she has to stay awhile after practice, since she'll be missing tomorrow's. I invite her to my place, since Matt will be at Bianca's tonight, and she shows up around nine looking nothing like my bright beauty. Her skin is sallow, tight lines tug her mouth down, and no trace of sparkle in her eyes. She slumps onto the couch with a wan smile.

"Tough practice?" I ask, sitting next to her, my body half-turned to face her.

"Tough day." She lets out a gust of breath. "I shouldn't have come. I'm physically and mentally drained right now. Coach is not happy I'm missing practice tomorrow, so I had to put in extra time."

"Don't go just yet," I say, putting my hand on her knee. "Want a glass of wine? Beer? Water?"

She squints her eyes at me for a moment. "How about some ice cream?"

"I think that's a great idea. Cal's is open until ten on Saturday nights."

She stands and reaches out her hand to help me up. "Buy me a scoop?"

"I'll buy you twenty if you want," I say with a grin.

We walk across the street hand-in-hand. It's busy, so we wait in line, not saying anything, just holding hands. Marnie clocks our hands and slides me a sly smile. "What can I getcha, hon?"

I raise my eyebrows at Palmer. She taps her lip with her finger as she evaluates the coolers. "How about a scoop of the double-double chocolate fudge on a sugar cone?"

"Just one scoop?" I ask.

Her nose crinkles. "My stomach isn't so settled. One scoop is plenty tonight."

I squeeze her hand and order my usual, twist cone, but add rainbow sprinkles. Marnie serves our order, and we head outside. Cal's outdoor patio is full, so we cross the street and sit on my stoop.

"What time are you leaving tomorrow?" I ask, licking the soft serve before it can melt in my hands. It's particularly humid tonight, and there's no breeze to move the stagnant air.

"First thing," she says. She licks the sides of her scoop, smoothing out the edges. "My mother wants me there before guests arrive, so around nine, I guess. The party starts at eleven."

"I can go with you," I offer, biting off the top of my cone.

She stares at her ice cream, which is starting to drip. I retrieve a napkin I'd stuck in my pocket and hand it to her. "Thanks. And thank you for offering, but I need to do this alone."

"Why?" My brows pinch together. "You don't have to do any of this alone, Palmer."

She nibbles at her cone. "I appreciate the gesture, Charlie.

But I don't want to subject you to my family drama. That's going above and beyond."

"It's what friends do for each other," I reply, choking down the words I really want to say. We're more than friends, and she knows it.

"You don't have to—"

"I want to. I'll pick you up at eight. Just tell me what to wear."

"No," she says on an exasperated breath. She stands up and walks to the curb to toss her half-eaten treat into the garbage can. She turns to face me with an unreadable expression. "You're not coming with me, Charlie."

"Why not?" I walk over and toss my cone away, too, so my hands are free to wrap around her shoulders.

"Because I don't want you to, Charlie." She rolls her shoulders, knocking my hands free. My arms dangle while I try to figure out what the hell is going on with her, why she's refusing my help. Refusing me. Then she takes a shot right at my heart.

"This isn't a relationship. It's a fling. You don't take the guy you're sleeping with to be your date to your cousin's engagement lunch, especially when she's engaged to your ex-boyfriend. My mother would know this wasn't real in a minute, and the last thing I need is to look even more pathetic."

I stumble back, the wind whipped right out of me. Slack-jawed, all I can do is stare at her. Her back is to me and she doesn't even realize she's just plunged a fucking stake through my heart. I grind my teeth, torn between scooping her up and taking her inside to show her exactly how real this is to me, and respecting her space.

"Why?" I croak, clearing my throat.

"Why what?" she asks, still not turning around.

"Why would your mother know in a minute I wasn't your boyfriend?" The words scrape my throat on the way out. I think I understand, but I need to hear it from Palmer.

She turns, her gaze sliding by me. Her chest flushes, tiny spots of rose bloom on cheeks visible by the streetlight. "She would just... know."

"Because I'm not like your previous boyfriends." I clench my jaw, every muscle in my body tensing. "I'm not rich or polished. I don't come from money or privilege. I'm not your type, right? I'm just a fun distraction."

"It's not—," she blows out a breath and casts a glance to the sky, setting her hands on her hips. "I'm not exactly your type, either, right?"

"What type is that?" I match her stance.

"Uh, let's see." She starts ticking things off with her fingers. "No more than five-foot-nothing in stocking feet, tiny ass, delicate bone structure, boobs you could fit in a wine glass."

"Bullshit," I say, although she just described Angela. And Liberty. And the flight attendant. Shit. I did have a type. At least I did before Palmer.

"You even have the same script, for God's sake. Don't pretend to be offended."

"What's that supposed to mean?"

"Oh, come on, Charlie," she scoffs. She holds up her fingers crooked like quotation marks. "'I'm so lucky to be with you.' 'I wish you believed how beautiful you are.' Give me a break. I know they're just lines. Liberty told me."

I rear back. "Liberty told you what? I honestly have no idea what the fuck you're talking about."

For a moment, her gaze wavers, and she seems unsure. But then she does that thing where she straightens her shoulders and steels herself, like she's going into battle. "Liberty warned me about the lines you use. She said you've said those exact words to her."

"She's lying," I protest. "I might have a few lines, I admit it. I liked to pick up women and take them home. It's mutual, all part of the little dance we do. But I've never said anything to you I didn't mean."

Her laugh is scornful. "She repeated them verbatim. How would she know exactly what you said to me, word-for-word, if you never said the same to her?"

"I don't know. I only know I meant those words for you and only you, Palmer."

She's breathing heavy, hands on her hips. She drops her head. "It doesn't matter. This isn't real. It never was. It never was supposed to be."

A cleat to my balls would hurt less. I don't know what to say, because I don't know what happened. I don't know what this is. A break-up? Can't break up something that doesn't exist, and according to her, nothing exists between us.

"I should go," she says, so quietly I almost don't hear her.

"Yeah. Maybe you should." I inch backward toward my house.

She looks up, her expression pinched, and takes a step toward me. "I'm sorry. I don't want to fight. You've become one of my closest friends, and I don't want to lose you."

I force a tight-lipped smile at her, even as the dagger twists in my heart. "Yeah. Well, I'll just wish you good luck tomorrow, then."

She takes another step forward while I retreat. "Can we—can I see you tomorrow? This thing is at eleven and I plan to get out of there as soon as I've eaten. Then can we talk about this? I'm just in a stupid mood, and I took it out on you, and I didn't mean it. I'm sorry. Please forgive me."

She comes to me. This time, I stand still and let her put her arms around me, her head fitting perfectly in the crook of my neck. I close my eyes and breathe in her sweet scent. I'll never be able to smell a peach the same way again. "Nothing to forgive. I'm sorry I pushed."

"Still friends?" she murmurs. Her breath ghosts over my fluttering pulse.

"Always," I say, struggling to keep my voice from cracking. I think I just lost the game. My chest is heavy. I've lost Palmer.

THIRTY

palmer

I DON'T SLEEP WELL after I leave Charlie's. Something happened between us that was both monumental and not good. He was genuinely hurt I didn't want him to come with me, and when I think about what I'd said, I realize how callous I'd come across. I'd all but told him he wasn't good enough to be my boyfriend. It's not true. I would be proud to call Charlie mine, despite what my parents might say, if I thought he felt the same. And my judgment is so off, I can't risk believing he might without proof.

By the time my alarm goes off, I've managed to capture a few hours of sleep. I shower, take care with my hair and makeup, and put on the daisy-patterned vintage swing dress I'd thrifted during a shopping excursion with Tisha.

"Ugh." I check the clock. If I don't leave in the next five minutes, I'll be late, and I'll never hear the end of it. I sling my little purse across my chest, grab my phone, and start for the door when I remember I forgot to put on the large pink daisy earrings I'd found to go with my dress. I set everything down, run to the bedroom to find them, then gather it all up and rush to the car.

Traffic is thankfully light heading west and I make it to my parents in just under an hour. Pretty sure I'll have a ticket in the mail thanks to the new speed camera they put up just past Exit 80, but it's a small price to pay to not face my mother's censure on top of everything else happening today.

I park in the side driveway as usual and make my way through the back door. I'm greeted with a bear hug from Helen. "Sweet girl," Helen says, pulling away. "You shouldn't be here. I don't know what your mother is thinking."

Tears suddenly spring to my eyes, and I'm grateful there is one person on my side here. "You know how she is."

"I do, which is why I told her she could fire me if she wants, but I will not be catering this engagement lunch."

My eyes widen. "What did she say?"

Helen picks up a rag and returns to wiping the counter. "I'm still here and there's a catering company setting up a big tent outside."

"Could've ordered pizzas and been done with it," I laugh.

"I did suggest getting a sub platter from Wegman's, which I still think is more than those people deserve."

I wrap my arms around Helen's waist and give her another squeeze. "Thanks, Helen."

She pats my arm. "Don't let the bastards get you down."

A genuine laugh bubbles out. Maybe I will survive this all.

I don't see my mother or father anywhere, so I use this temporary moment of peace to gather my wits about me. I steal into the family room and have a seat, reaching for my phone and coming up empty. *Shit.* I think I left it on my kitchen counter when I went back to retrieve the earrings. Guess I won't be able to call for help.

My reprieve is short-lived. Mom pokes her head in the room, then seeing me, comes in and shuts the pocket door behind her.

"I didn't realize you'd already arrived. You can't hide out all day, Palmer."

"I was merely gathering my energy before the hordes descend."

"Do you think, for today, you could brush the chip off your shoulder? I don't expect you to do it for Rania or Brennan, but I'd appreciate it if you'd do it for me."

She purses her lips, painted a subtle shade of coral that matches the short-sleeved sweater set she wears. "I'm not happy with Rania, but she's my only niece, and family must forgive family."

I've heard some version of that my whole life, and I am sick of it. "Even when family stabs you in the back the way she did?"

"I understand your anger and I agree it's justified," she says. She perches on the edge of the sofa cushion next to me.

"Then why are you doing this? Why throw them an engagement party and make me come for it?"

"It's the right thing to do to show everyone there are no hard feelings."

My laugh is more of a cackle, but I can't help myself. "Oh, but there are hard feelings."

"But we don't have to show them—"

"Why not?" I stand, a fire catching in my stomach. "Nowadays, this wouldn't even rate a comment on Facebook."

"It's about appearances. You have no idea what it's like to be the subject of gossip and mockery. I do. I need you to do your part."

"This isn't healthy, Mom, and I can't keep doing this." I breathe in through my nose and exhale a resigned breath. "This one last time, I'll show my face, slap on a smile, and go through the motions. But do not expect me at the wedding, Mom. I mean it."

"I suppose that's fair."

"And you and Dad need to start coming to my games." I hold up a hand to stop whatever she's about to say. "You're all about appearances. Well, how do you think it looks when one of your clients knows more about your daughter and her career than you do? You don't have to approve of what I do. But I'd appreciate some support. Just like I'm showing my support for you today."

"All right. You make a good point." She stares, her gaze slipping down my dress until she zeroes in on my tattoo peeking out from under the hem. "Is that... a tattoo?"

I put my arm around her shoulders and guide her out of the room. "You can yell at me later, Mom. Appearances, remember?"

Workers set up a large white party tent in the back, where the guests will sit. Tables and chairs are being moved inside, while my parents' gardeners unload a pickup truck full of flowers. The kitchen has been taken over by servers arranging finger sandwiches and hors d'oeuvres on serving platters, and Helen is nowhere to be seen. I don't blame her.

When the valets arrive, I offer to help them set up along the drive, recalling how my mother has done it in the past. I finish giving directions and making sure they have shade and water, and start back to the house. I'm thinking about Charlie and wondering if I should try to call him from the house phone. I need to hear his voice. I don't like how things went last night, and it's all my fault. I'm lost in my thoughts, so I don't see the happy couple until I nearly bump into them.

"Palmer." My name on Rania's tongue is cloying. She opens her arms, but I step back, forcing her to drop them. She loops an arm through Brennan's and the two of them smile at me like idiots.

"Rania. Dickhead," I greet them.

Brennan gives me a pitying look. "Really? Name-calling? It's beneath you, Palmer."

"Actually, you're beneath me," I retort.

Rania looks me up and down, and I return the gesture. She's picture perfect; my mother will be pleased. Her platinum hair falls around her face in a cascade of curls. Her big blue eyes, a lighter shade than mine, glitter with contempt. She wears a light blue satiny, sleeveless sheath that falls to her knees, and a pair of beaded Prada slingbacks. I draw myself to my full height, determined not to let her make me feel insecure.

"Nice hair," Rania says with false sincerity. "Suits you."

"Thanks, I think so, too." I'm not taking the bait. As I stare at the two of them together, I feel nothing but a nagging sense of regret I ever wasted my time with this ass. I can't believe I ever thought being with Charlie would make me look desperate to these people. He's one-thousand times the man Brennan is and I'm an idiot for keeping him away.

"Well, the guests will start arriving soon," I say. "I'm sure you'll want to finish getting ready."

Rania touches her hair with a frown. "We are ready."

"Oh. Okay, then." I flash a fake smile and walk past them to the house. I steal a look over my shoulder, where Rania has opened a compact and is inspecting herself, while Brennan murmurs reassurances. I turn back before they catch me and snicker. Score one for the goalie.

I sit on the back deck with a mimosa I swiped from one of the catering trays, watching as guests trickle in. Rania and Brennan are somewhere in the house waiting for the cue for their big entrance.

The sliding door opens behind me and I'm pleasantly surprised it's Boone, wearing a tan summer-weight sport coat over a light green open-necked dress shirt. "There you are," he says.

I raise my glass. "Getting a head start."

"Me, too." He holds up a similar glass. "There's an entire tray back there. Should I grab it?"

I laugh. "I think we'll get more in the tent."

"Speaking of," he says, holding out his free hand. "Your mother asked me to find you and escort you to your seat."

I roll my eyes, but take his hand and let him help me up. "I guess it's time."

"How are you holding up?" His eyes hold compassion, and I'm grateful, even though a big part of me wishes Charlie were here.

"Fine. It turns out, I'm not all that angry anymore. More annoyed." I had told Boone about the breakup and Brennan's subsequent engagement. "I'm looking forward to the mini crab cakes, but otherwise, I just want this over. Playoffs are this week and I'm already missing today's practice."

We talk about the upcoming games as he escorts me to the tent. Before we enter to find our seats, he stops me and pulls a small box out of his pocket. "I brought this for you. Saw it online and it made me think of you."

"You didn't have to," I say. I open the box and find a red rope bracelet with a lacrosse stick charm holding two of the ends together. "I love it!"

"The rope they used is what the string the stick heads with." He takes it out of the box and loosens the fastening. I stick out my hand and he slips it on, tightening it. "I know you can't wear it during the game, but I hope it'll bring you some luck."

"Thank you. This is so thoughtful." I give him a hug and kiss him on the cheek.

"Maybe after the season is over and things aren't so crazy with the housing site, we can make some plans to see each other."

I bite my lip and look down at the bracelet. "Maybe."

"Unless there's someone else?" he asks, a half smile on his lips.

I open my mouth, ready to protest, but all I can do is shrug. "Maybe."

"Your friend, Charlie?"

I furrow my brow. "How'd you guess?"

"That night I took you to dinner, it was kind of obvious he was into you."

"Was it?"

"As obvious as it was you were into him."

I blush. "It's complicated."

"It usually is," Boone sighs.

I put my hand on Boone's chest. "I'm sorry."

"Don't be," he says, taking my hand and kissing my knuckles. "He's a lucky man. But I do hope we can still be friends. You're my only lacrosse connection, and I plan on hitting you up for tickets again."

I laugh. "Deal."

charlie

WHEN I ROLL out of bed Sunday morning, Matt and Bianca are in the kitchen making breakfast. Well, Bianca is flipping pancakes while Matt's hands roam all over her.

"Why are you guys here?" I grumble, opening the fridge for the orange juice. It's not where I last saw it, and when I check the recycle bin, I find the empty carton. "Christ, Matt. Buy your own fucking juice."

"Hey," Matt snaps, letting go of Bianca, whose face is somewhere between fuchsia and red. "What's your problem?"

"Sorry, Charlie," Bianca says, turning the pancakes over. "I had the last of it this morning. I'll pick up another carton."

I drop into a chair and run my hands over my face. "No, I'm sorry, B. You can help yourself anytime you want."

"We've got coffee," she says, pointing to the machine. "And extra pancakes."

"Not hungry, thanks. But I'll take you up on your offer of coffee."

"What the fuck is wrong with you?" Matt asks, taking a mug out of the cabinet and filling it with coffee. He plants it down in front of me, some of the hot liquid splashing over the sides. "You look like shit."

"Thanks." I take a long drink of the black coffee and wince. It needs a splash of cream, but I don't care to get up. "Seriously, though. Why are you here?" I thought I'd get the day to mope and figure out what to do about Palmer.

"We're spending the day at Rocky Point," Bianca says. "We came back to pick up the beach chairs and pack a lunch."

"We'll be out of your hair soon." Matt holds out a plate so Bianca can flip the finished pancakes onto it. "Why, is your girl coming over?"

"She's not my girl," I mumble into my mug.

I don't miss the subtle glance between my brother and his fiancée. "You want to talk about it?" he asks.

Bianca turns off the griddle. "I can leave you two alone to talk. I'll just take my pancake out to the back porch."

"No, no. It's fine." I wave her down in a chair. "We had a disagreement last night, and some things were said. I guess whatever I've been doing over the past couple of months hasn't meant anything to her."

"Did she say that?" Bianca asks, dousing her pancakes in the specialty maple syrup she gets from Homegoods, then pushing the bottle of Mrs. Butterworth toward my brother.

"Sort of." I wave my hand in the air. "It's a little hazy. I got drunk after she left."

"What did she say?" Matt adds a pat of butter to his stack, then reaches over and drops one on top of Bianca's. So in sync with one another, it kills me.

"She has a family thing," I explain. "A fucked up family thing. Her ex is marrying her cousin, and there's an engagement party today her mother is hosting. Palmer's been bullied into attending."

Bianca huffs. "That's insane. What kind of mother does

173

that to their daughter? If she's hosting anything, it should be a barbeque to flambe that guy's nuts."

"So what are you gonna do about it?" Matt asks.

"I offered to go with her. She told me no."

"Why?" Matt mumbles around a bite of pancake.

"Chew, swallow, talk, babe," Bianca says. I smirk behind the lip of my mug.

"She dates guys that wear Armani and get $200 hair-cuts." I run a hand through my hair. "Mom's friend Rosie cuts my hair and the closest I get to wearing designer is what's on sale at Men's Wearhouse. She said everyone would know I wasn't her real boyfriend and that'd make her look more desperate than if she went alone."

Matt winces. He takes a drink of his coffee. "Yikes."

"I'm sure she didn't mean it the way it sounded," Bianca says, though her voice is uncertain.

I grunt. "Not much to interpret there. If she can't see me as a potential mate by now, how much hope is there? We agreed to do this for the season, which is over in a week if the Battle bomb out of the playoffs or three weeks if they make it all the way. It doesn't help that fucking Liberty got in her head."

"Who's Liberty?" Bianca asks.

"A girl Charlie works with. He hooked up with her when he first started and it didn't end well. Think bunny boiling."

"She's not crazy," I insist. "But she's still pissed. She convinced Palmer everything I've ever said to her is part of a script I use to charm women into bed."

"Looks like you got your work cut out for you," Matt says.

"Why bother?" I snort. "It's done. I failed."

"Damn, Charlie," Bianca says, pointing her fork at me. "I didn't realize you were such a quitter."

"I'm a realist," I grouse.

"You know what you need?" Bianca asks.

"A lobotomy."

"No, a grand gesture." Bianca looks between Matt and me as we stare at her with blank faces. "You know? The big moment in a rom-com when one of the main characters expresses their undying love, either through some big speech or a grand romantic gesture. Like when Hugh Grant saves the Community Center for Sandra Bullock in *Two Weeks Notice*?"

My brother and I exchange a quick look. "Yeah, babe," Matt says. "I don't think we've seen it."

Bianca grunts in frustration. "It's our next movie night. Fine. I'll spell it out. GO. GET. THE. GIRL. Ride up on a white horse and rescue her. Be her Knight in Shining Armor. Bring her flowers. Hold a boombox outside her window. Do something."

"You think I should go to her parents' house and crash the party?" My mind is starting to turn with possibilities.

"Yup."

"What if I get there and she turns me away?"

"Would you be any worse off than you are now?" Matt sits back with his arm hooked over the back of the chair. "*Carlito*, at this point, you're either going to be crushed or get everything you wanted. You're well past the point of no return with Palmer. So either fish or cut bait. Stop fucking around."

I hate it when my brother's right. The game isn't over yet. There's still time on the clock for me to make a move. Speaking of clocks... *shit*. "The party starts in less than an hour."

"Then you better hurry," Bianca says, shooing me out of the kitchen.

I race out of the kitchen, then stop and swing back to plant a loud smacker on Bianca's lips. "Thanks, future sis."

I cackle as I run to my room before my brother can kick

my ass. I have to clean myself up quick. There's a party I gotta crash. Right after I make a quick stop at the florist.

Finding a florist open on Sunday is impossible, so I settle for a bouquet of daisies and sunflowers from the grocery store and haul ass to Frederick. There's a speed camera along the way, so I expect a ticket in the mail, but she's worth it. I follow the GPS up a mountain road surrounded by forest, almost sure I've gotten lost, when a huge estate spreads out before me.

I turn into the long driveway and spot the young men in valet uniforms watching over rows of luxury vehicles parked in a roped-off area along the side. My Honda Civic is fully loaded, but it's no Lexus. I pull over before I reach the top of the drive and hike the rest of the way.

I'm not sure where to go. Music and voices are coming from the back of the house, but should I ring the bell? Or just walk in. I've never crashed a party before, so I don't know the appropriate protocol. I approach a guy in black pants, white button-down, and tie, carrying a foil tray from a catering van.

"Excuse me," I call out. "You wouldn't happen to know where I could find Palmer York, would you?"

"Is she one of the waitresses? Probably making rounds of drinks. Hey, grab one of the bags of ice, will you?"

"I'm not staff," I say, glancing down at my charcoal trousers. With my white button-down and red and black tie, I could pass for catering staff. Great.

"Oh, sorry." Hands full, he nods toward the back of the house. "Everyone is just getting seated, so I assume back there. They'll be announcing the couple soon, so you might want to hurry and find your seat."

"Thanks." Flowers in hand, I head in the direction he pointed, stopping to hold open the gate for him and slipping in behind. As I look around the small crowd, an older woman in a sweater set complete with pearls approaches.

"Oh no," she says, pointing at the flowers. "We didn't order daisies. You can take this away."

"I don't—" I stammer. What the hell is she talking about?

"I'm sorry, I don't speak Mexican." She taps the bouquet and makes a shooing motion. "No flores." Only she pronounces it "flor-izz."

The eyes are a dead giveaway this is Palmer's mother. Before I can try to tell her again I'm not staff, and I can speak English, she walks off. I spot Palmer. She's hard to miss in that short, form-fitting dress she's wearing; she's not only a standout but a knockout. My heart starts pumping in earnest while I watch her. She's with that joker from the game, the rich guy with the dumb name. Bone or something? I clench the flowers in my hand, the plastic wrap crinkling beneath my fingers.

He hands her something. I can't make out what it is, but the smile on her face could make the sun jealous. She gives him a kiss and he holds her hand. My stomach bottoms out as they head into the tent. He pulls out a chair for her and then sits next to her. I swallow hard.

That's why she didn't want me to come. She already had a date for this, and unlike me, this guy wouldn't be mistaken for the hired help. I walk out the way I came in, passing the same guy as before.

"You find her?"

"Lost her, actually." I toss the flowers onto the lawn and keep striding past him, past the valets, and back to my car. It's done now.

THIRTY-TWO

LUNCH WAS ABOUT AS uneventful as it could be. With the company of the Wainwrights, time passed quickly, and their presence tempered my mother's attitude. The raspberry and lemon trifles were to die for, and the only reason I stayed through dessert. I snag a couple on my way out to share with Charlie. Since I left a little later than I thought I would, I drive straight to his place instead of stopping at my apartment to pick up my phone. I don't think I'll need it anyway.

I luck out and find parking along the street only a few doors down. With the dessert in hand, I flounce up the stairs to his place. We need to talk. I have to tell him I was wrong. I'm not cut out for casual sex or easy hookups, and I can't change. Moreover, I don't want to change. Because I've completely fallen for Charlie, and I think he might feel the same. I don't care what Liberty said about his insincerity. I'm not even sure I believe her anymore. Charlie was so adamant last night, and why shouldn't I believe him? He's never lied to me. He's never let me down.

I ring the bell and bounce on the balls of my feet while I wait for him to answer. When he does, the smile spread across my face falters. His hair is sticking up on one side of his head, his eyes bloodshot. He stares at me like he can't figure out who I am or what I'm doing here.

"Palmer?"

Ah, he knows who I am. "Can I come in?" When he hesitates, I hold up the little bag with the trifles in it. "I have dessert."

He sighs, then steps back and swings the door open. I enter, noting the empty cans of Natty on the table. I set the bag down next to them and face him. He shuts the door and shoves his hands into his pockets. He's wearing a pair of trousers and a white dress shirt completely unbuttoned to reveal a tight tee. I drink in his well-defined muscles and the dark, smooth span of skin along the hollow of his neck. My libido stirs, my breathing quickening. I drag my gaze to his dark and hooded eyes.

"I thought we could talk about last night," I say, forcing myself to focus. Before we get down to any fun, there's important business to take care of.

"You sure that's what you want?" he says in a husky voice. "To talk? Because you're looking at me like I'm the dessert."

"I mean," I lick my lips, "I can't really help it. But yes, we should talk. Probably."

He saunters toward me. His finger traces down the side of my face, and he grasps my chin hard, pulling down to open my mouth. He slants his lips over mine, and I taste the beer, but I also taste Charlie. My Charlie. I open wider and he deepens the kiss. I rub against him, feeling his thick cock against my thighs. We can talk later.

He walks me backward, carefully guiding me around the table, until we reach the sectional. My knees buckle when I hit the cushion and he falls forward on top of me, biting my lips and my ear and the side of my neck. He stops for a moment to shed his shirts, and I rake my nails up and down his gorgeous chest, dragging my fingers along the ridges of his abs to the button of his pants. In seconds, I free him from the confines of his clothes. He pushes my dress up and yanks my panties down.

"How wet are you?" He hisses against my chest. He licks in the valley between my breasts while his fingers slide through my folds. "Always so wet. For me? Is this for me?"

"Yesss," I pant. "All yours."

I spread my legs wide, inviting him inside my heat. He ducks his head and licks a long trail from my entrance up through my sensitive lips to my clit, then stares at me and draws the back of his hand across his mouth. I can't explain why I find it so sexy, but my need blazes.

He pulls me onto his lap. I rise and use my hand to grip him so I can lower myself onto his shaft, but he stops me. He leans over to retrieve his wallet and extracts a condom. I look at him, confused, because I thought this was something we'd agreed on.

He doesn't look at me as he tears open the packet and rolls it on. He fists his cock and lines it up to my entrance. I'm so hungry for him, I don't wait and impale myself on him. We both hiss as he slides balls deep into me. I start to move, using his shoulders for purchase, as I bounce up and down, trying to shift myself into the position I need for maximum pleasure. He rolls me onto my back, never breaking the connection, and hikes one leg up on his shoulder. I shriek as he pounds inside me, touching me exactly where I need. I arch my back and shout his name as the first wave crests over me. He pushes and pushes, sweat pouring off his body.

"This is what you wanted, right?" he growls. "You just want me to fuck you. Fuck you and make you come harder than you'll ever fucking come again. You hear me? I'm the only one who will ever fuck you this good."

"Oh, God! Yes, Charlie, yes. Only you, only you." I gulp air, trying to force my lungs to expand. But the need is crushing me, stealing my breath. I dig my nails into his back until he yells.

"I can't fucking stop."

"Don't," I keen. "I'm coming, Charlie."

I tighten my legs around his hips and he pumps into me in three long, devastating strokes. He lets out a wail that blends with my own until I don't know whose echo I'm hearing in my head.

After several long moments, he holds the condom and pulls slowly out of me. Boneless, I lie staring at the ceiling, blinking away the fuzzy gray dots floating above me while he takes care of the cleanup.

"Charlie," I say, but my voice is creaky. I want to tell him right now how I feel. I'm madly in love with him and I'm bursting to say it. I have to tell him, no matter what the consequences. I sit up and find my panties, slipping back into them.

Charlie comes back wearing a pair of low-slung shorts and an unreadable expression. He leans against the door jamb and cracks open another can of beer. "Did you say something?"

I startle at the brusque way he speaks. "Is everything okay?"

He takes a sip and stares at me. "Yeah. Everything's fine."

"You're acting weird."

"Am I?"

His voice is flat, cold even. I wrap my arms around my middle. "What's wrong?"

"Nothing." He sighs and straightens. "Is there something else you wanted to do? Something else I could teach you?"

My mouth hangs open. I stand on still-unsteady legs. "Why are you acting like this?"

"Like what?"

"Like a dick, that's what."

He raises an eyebrow. "How am I a dick?"

"How are you—" I run my hands through my hair. "We just made love and you're acting like it was nothing."

"We didn't make love, Palmer. We fucked. Like we have been doing. Like you wanted me to show you how to do, remember? Sex without love, something you'd never done before. Well, sweetheart, it's called fucking."

My heart stutters and tears spring to my eyes. I rub the sore spot on my chest. "I don't understand why you're acting like this."

He runs a hand down his face. "We had a deal. I would show you what it's like to have a fling, as you call it. How to date someone, fuck them, without getting attached. I think we're at the end of your lessons. You need to concentrate on the playoffs, and I need to—"

"What?" I tilt my head and glare at him. "You need to what?"

He looks away. "I need to get back to my life."

My body sways. I'm physically ill right now. I can't believe I was about to admit I loved him. God. He just saved me from making the same mistake I've been making my whole life. Maybe he sensed it and this is his way of stopping me before I made a complete fool of myself.

"Right." I dig in the bag with the trifles and take out my wallet and keys. "Enjoy the mini trifles. You should put them in the fridge if you aren't going to eat them right away."

My sandals had come off around the time he pushed me down on the couch, and it took me a brief search to find where

I'd kicked them under the table. I put them on and walk to the door, careful not to go near him. My hand on the knob, I stop.

"Why the condom?" I asked.

His jaw tightens. "We said we'd skip them, but only as long as it was just you and me."

I close my eyes against the pain rocketing through my chest, then fling the door open and rush outside before I break. I barely make it to my car before the dam bursts and the tears begin flowing from my shattered heart.

THIRTY-THREE

I'M HAVING A SHITTY PRACTICE. And everyone knows it.

"York," Coach Arkhady bellows. "Pull your head out of your ass. My niece does a better job in goal than you are today, and she's a six-year-old who doesn't know her left from right."

"Yes, Coach."

I don't improve much the rest of the day, which ends up being one of the longest of my life. The coaches keep me after practice, drilling me repeatedly, until I stop looking like a U10 rookie out there. Every muscle aches, though not as much as my heart. I forgo the therapy pool and take a quick shower, anxious to go home and soak in my tub.

Tisha is waiting for me at my car when I leave. The look on her face is so kind, I want to sob. Or punch something. My mood right now could go either way. "If you stuck around to tell me to pull it together, you can save your breath. I know."

"I know you know. Just like I know Coach has already chewed you a new one, so you don't need me to do it."

I unlock my door, but she remains leaning against it. "I'm exhausted, T. Can we talk tomorrow?"

"That's what you said on Monday. And Tuesday. And Wednesday. Well, girl, now it's Thursday and we have a game tomorrow. A pretty important one. I don't think we can push this talk off any longer."

I nod once. "Where's your car?" I look around, but I don't see her Camaro.

"Manny dropped me off. I brought a sleepover bag." She lifts a small duffel I didn't see before. "But no alcohol."

"I know, big game tomorrow."

I drive her back to my apartment, spending the time together rehashing strategy and discussing the first play-off game tomorrow. It's not until we're settled in, pajamas on, ESPN2 on for background noise, that she asks me the dreaded question.

"What happened to you and Charlie?"

"It's over." I tell her the whole story, much of it she already knew about, filling in details here and there. When I get to the events of the past weekend, I'm able to hold it together until the very end.

"When I got home, I had a text from him I hadn't seen since I didn't have my phone on me all day. It explains why he looked confused when I showed up. It basically said something came up and he wasn't going to be free for a while."

But it wasn't something. It was some*one*. Otherwise, why would we go back to using a condom on our last night?

"I did it again," I sob into her shoulder. "I let my heart get involved. I didn't learn a damn thing and I'm pretty sure I've lost one of my best friends in the process."

"Hey, hey, hey." Tisha strokes my hair. "You did learn something. You learned how to stand up to your parents. You learned how beautiful and strong you are. You learned your limits. So don't go thinking this was a pointless exercise."

I hiccup. "I just feel so awful. I've never felt this bad before.

Not after Brennan dumped me. Not after any of my other boyfriends, all of whom I was planning futures with. So why does it hurt so much when I went into this knowing there was no future with Charlie? It wasn't until that last night when I realized how much I loved him that I even entertained the notion he could possibly love me back. So why does this hurt so fucking much?"

Tisha sighs. "Maybe because this is the first time you truly loved someone. All those other times you thought you were in love. You complained to me that you always fell too hard, too fast. Did you fall for Charlie on Day One?"

I hiccup again. "N-no."

"See?" she says. "This wasn't a burn-fast-and-hot shooting star. That's why this hurts so much."

"What do I do now?" I ask Tisha.

"Right now? You let this thing between you two breathe. Play your heart out for the team. Put all your energy and focus in the goal and on leading your defense. And when you're done, you're gonna knock on that man's door and you're gonna tell him exactly how you feel about him. Put it all on the line, come what may."

"And if he rejects me? Again?" I sniffle.

"Then we'll go get drunk and I'll help you pick up the pieces."

I laugh and tip my head to her shoulder. "Thanks, Tisha. I don't know what I'd do without you."

"That's what friends are for. Now let's get to bed. We've got an ass-whooping to hand out to Denver tomorrow night."

I take Tisha's advice and put Charlie out of my mind, pouring my entire heart and soul into the playoffs. When we make it to the Championship Game, I call my parents and invite them to come out to watch, even though it means traveling to New Jersey to play Philadelphia on a neutral field. To my surprise, both of them say yes.

I haven't seen Charlie all week. Someone mentioned he'd been working more up in the office or in the broadcast booth. But I have a feeling I'll see him tonight at this final game. I try not to think about it as we go through our pregame rituals. My focus is on the game one last time.

Coach Arkhady fires us up, and we emerge from the tunnel ready to take on the Stars. I look over to where friends and families are seated, and see my parents sitting with the Wainwrights. I lift my stick in a wave and they cheer. Even my mother.

After the anthem, we take our positions on the field. At the draw, Philly takes possession and makes a fast break. But we're ready, and the opponent takes a shot that bounces off the right post and is picked up by Marisol. She makes a quick pass to Ava, who takes it down to the opposite arc. After a few passes, Allie takes a shot, sending it perfectly into the net. We've drawn first blood. I bang the posts with my stick, my teammates on and off the field shouting in celebration. I lock in and prepare for the next draw.

It's a fast-paced game and we're evenly matched. After our first few goals, Philly finds its stride and begins matching us goal for goal. At halftime, Philly has cut our lead down to three. I'm following everyone out of the locker room when I spot Charlie and my heart somersaults. He doesn't see me, so I hang back and drink him in. He looks the same as ever. I can't see who he's speaking with, but when he smiles, I'm blindsided. Whoever it is gets the two-dimple treatment. A beautiful brunette steps into view to reach up on tiptoe and kiss his cheek. I'm not surprised, but another piece of my heart chips off and floats away. I can't afford to stand here anymore. I snap on my helmet and rush out to the field to take my place.

The second half is grueling. I'm peripherally aware Charlie's on the sidelines now, but my focus is where it should be—on the field. Our lead is down to one with only a minute left on the clock. Ava makes a shot brilliantly blocked by the Stars' goalie. She clears it across field to a player who'd been sitting in my blind spot on the right. The attacker moves across the arc.

"Cutter!" I shout.

My defense is on it and she takes a shot easily deflected. But the ref blows her whistle. "Shooting space," she calls.

It's a penalty on us. Andi put her body in the path of the attacker, resulting in our opponent being awarded a free shot from the 8-meter arc. "I'm sorry," Andi pants, hands on her knees.

"It's all right. Shake it off." I bang each of my posts and crouch into position. Andi moves behind the attacker and defense lines up along the arc, ready to crash the net. I draw in a few deep breaths to center myself.

I study the Philly player's shoulders for any indication if she's going high or low with the shot. The whistle blows. She angles left, her shoulders coming up. I straighten slightly and move my focus to the head of her stick to anticipate the release. One step, two steps... she swings her stick, the bright yellow ball coming at me. My eyes are on it, and working on instinct, I push out in time for it to bounce off the side of my stick head. It drops down and I scoop it up on the ricochet.

The crowd noise is deafening. The clock winds down. I wait until the last possible second before stepping out of the crease and into the arc. Swinging my eyes back and forth, I look for someone open to take the clear, but Philly covers our players like ants on a picnic sandwich. I run toward center field, keeping my cradle tight, dodging checks from the opponents. Someone calls my name and I find Allie, who's shaken her defender behind the opposite net. I rear back and push my stick forward, sending the ball sailing. She catches it and wraps the crease, dumping it in behind the goalie before the other woman has time to react.

This whistle blows, signifying the goal just as the horn announces the end of the game. We've done it. We're the league champions.

I catch Charlie's eye during all the celebrating on the field, which he is, of course, capturing for the socials. He grins widely and gives me a thumbs up. I smile back and shake my stick.

"Too bad we won't be enjoying his flavor of eye candy next season," Jewel sighs next to me.

"What do you mean?" I ask.

"I heard he's transferring to the Red Hawks. I think someone said he's moving back to Annapolis."

I spin around, my heart in my throat, but now I can't find him. The crowd has swallowed him up.

palmer

IT'S a while before I'm finally released. Everyone is heading back to the hotel and then out to a local club to celebrate, even the coaches. I look for my parents as we walk out to the bus and spot them waiting with the Wainwrights. I jog over and my father envelops me in a tight hug.

"Congratulations," he says. "I'm so proud of you."

"It was a great game," Ned Wainwright says, and everyone echoes the sentiment.

"Thanks," I say, pulling out of my dad's arms and kissing my mom on the cheek. "Thank you for coming," I say to her.

"Sorry it took so long," she says, squeezing my hand. "I won't pretend I understood anything that was going on out there, but still—well done, Palmer."

"Are you guys going back to the hotel?" I ask.

"I think we decided to drive home," my dad says. "It's only a few hours, and your mother would rather be in her own bed."

"Me, too," Patsy agrees.

"And I'm the official driver," Boone says. He hugs me. "You looked great out there."

"What about that save in the second quarter?" my dad and Ned begin rehashing some of my finer moments. I look over to see Charlie loading gear into the trunk of a car parked near the bus.

"Sorry, I have to go. I'll call you tomorrow." I kiss my mother on the cheek and say goodbye to every-one. "Thanks again for coming."

My teammates are still milling about the bus and the managers continue to load on the equipment. I have at least a few minutes and I can't put this off any longer.

"Hi." I strive to keep my voice even as I approach.

He looks up and straightens. "Hi."

"How have you been?" My heart races worse than when I was on the field.

"Fine. You looked good out there," he says. A grin splits his beautiful face. "I knew you'd kill it."

"I'm glad one of us did," I joke, letting out a nervous chuckle. "So, um, I heard you're moving? Is it true?"

His smile dulls. "Matt and Bianca are going to be moving in together. I figured I'd give them space."

"But Annapolis? You're leaving the Battle, too?"

He puts his hands on his hips and stares at the ground. "It's time to move on."

My stomach rolls. "Is it because of me?"

His eyes sparkle with so much emotion when he looks at me it physically hurts to keep staring at him. "It's for a lot of reasons. I transferred here because Pete's parents—he's my former best friend—"

"I remember. You walked in on him and your girlfriend."

His cheeks flush. "Right. Anyway, they live next door to my parents, and I was always stressed out about running into him or Angela whenever I was home. I wanted to make a clean break. It's been five years. It's time. I don't care if

I run into them. They don't have the power to hurt me anymore."

"That's good," I say. "I'm glad for you."

We stare at each other, a million things needing to be said falling in a silent, unspoken heap between us. He looks over my shoulder, his jaw ticking. "I see your parents came. You must feel good about it."

I glance over to where they're having an animated conversation with Coach Arkhady. My mother is actually laughing, something I wasn't sure she knew how to do. "Yeah. Ever since the engagement party, they've been trying harder to be more supportive."

He grunts. "And I see your boyfriend's here. I'm happy you found someone who appreciates what you do. You deserve that."

My face scrunches. "Boyfriend? Do you mean Boone? I told you, he's just a friend."

Charlie blows out a harsh breath. "Come on, Palmer. I saw you two."

"When?" I rack my brain trying to remember the last time I saw Boone before tonight. It was at the engagement lunch, but Charlie wasn't there.

"I went to your parents' house to crash the engagement party and rescue you, but apparently you didn't need rescuing. Met your mother, by the way. She thought I was part of the non-English speaking staff." He nods over at Boone. "You two looked pretty cozy. I know he's the kind of guy you imagine having a life with and, as your mother unintentionally made obvious, better suited to your life than I would be. I hope I was able to help you get what you wanted and that he treats you like the Goddess you are. You deserve nothing less, Palmer."

"What are you talking about?" I take a step closer to

him. "There's nothing but friendship between Boone and me, Charlie. Whatever you think you saw, you got it wrong."

His gaze flickers. "I saw you kiss him, Palmer."

"He gave me a gift. I thanked him." I put a hand on Charlie's arm. His muscles tense under my touch. "Is this why—"

"Palmer. Hey."

I drop my hand and take a step back, plastering a smile on my face. "Hi, Matt. Thanks for coming to the game."

The pretty brunette next time nudges his arm, and I recognize her from earlier with Charlie. "This is my fiancée, Bianca."

Matt's *fiancée*. Relief flows through me. I reach out a hand. "Lovely to meet you."

"Likewise," she says, shaking my hand. "I've heard so much about you. Charlie talks about you endlessly."

"Really?" I glance at Charlie, who's rubbing the back of his neck and looking distinctly uncomfortable.

"I wouldn't say endlessly," Matt interjects, coming to his brother's rescue. "No more so than any of the other women he knows."

"Matt," Charlie warns.

"York," shouts Coach Arkhady. "Bus is moving out. Let's roll!"

"Better go. I know everyone's going out tonight. You don't want to miss it." Charlie shuts the trunk.

"Will you be joining us?" I ask.

"I don't know," he says, juggling the keys in his palm. "Dante, Mei, and Liberty are going. So maybe."

Matt opens the back door for his fiancée and helps her into the car. "Nice meeting you, Palmer," she says before ducking her head inside.

"You, too, Bianca. Good luck with the wedding."

Matt shuts the door and shoots Charlie a look. "Take care, Palmer. Congrats on the game."

"Thanks." I stare at Charlie for another long moment, trying to read his expression. "Charlie—"

"You should hurry. They're waiting on you." He jerks his chin at me. "See you around, Palmer."

He gets in the car and doesn't look back. So I do the only thing I can do. I let him go.

charlie

"LET'S GO, let's go, let's go!" Dante claps his hands. "Everyone's already at the club."

"I'm not going," I say, staring up at the ceiling from where I lie on the hotel bed. Matt and Bianca went back to their room. They're making a weekend of it, so Dante and I are sharing a room and will drive back together tomorrow. "I should work on content, so I don't have to spend all of tomorrow doing it."

"Dude, that's why we have interns." Dante plops down on the edge of the bed, the pants of his dark purple drainpipe pants riding up to show his bare ankles. They don't look the least bit comfortable, but what do I know about fashion? "Since you're going to be leaving us for the dark side, the least you can do is come out and celebrate with us."

"It's the men's team. I'll still be around. Just not in Baltimore."

"That's what I'm sayin'," Dante says. He looks thoughtful. "If it's Liberty, I'll run interference."

I roll my eyes. "It's not Liberty. We're in a truce right now, anyway."

"Great." He jumps. "Then there's nothing stopping you from being the Goose to my Maverick."

"You know Goose died in that movie."

"Yeah, but not before he helped Maverick get the girl."

I swing my legs over the side of the bed and sigh. "All right. But if you pick a girl up, you're going back to her place. I'm not giving up my bed."

"Aye, aye, cap'n." Dante salutes. "Let's move it on out."

We arrive at the club some time after everyone else has gotten there. The dance floor is packed, mostly with members of the Baltimore Battle. We quickly find our little group at a table off in the corner.

I scan the area but don't see Palmer, which is probably a good thing. I believe her when she says she isn't dating that guy, but it doesn't matter, does it? I'm still not in her league, and I never will be. I'm Charming Charlie, always up for a good time. A fun distraction. Dante gets us a couple of shots and Palomas to start with. I down my shot in one go, wincing at the burn of the tequila down my throat.

"So Charlie," Mei says. "When do you make the move to Annapolis?"

"Later this summer," I reply, shouting to be heard over the music. "It hasn't been finalized yet."

"We'll miss you," Emma says. "I've learned so much under you."

"It was a pleasure working with you. I've already given my recommendations to JJ for you and Benji."

Her face lights up and she lifts her martini in a salute. "You're the best."

Benji shows up, sweaty hair sticking to his head. "Come on, Em. They're playing our song."

She takes his hand and follows him out to the dance floor, where a dance mix of a OneRepublic hit blares from the speakers. "I must be getting old because the thought of going out there to dance is enough to give me a headache."

"Don't worry, old man," Dante says. "I'll find you a walker if your gout starts acting up."

"Fuck off," I laugh.

Jewel, who plays offense for the Battle, taps Dante on the shoulder. Pink glitter lashes highlight her deep brown eyes, the bright magenta of her lips a mesmerizing contrast to her rich-brown skin. I've never seen her without her hair tucked into an unobtrusive sleek bun or ponytail, but tonight her mane falls in shiny black curls down to her shoulders. She's a knockout, a fact Dante obviously notes.

"Hey, Dante. Wanna dance?" she asks, the light glinting off the tiny diamond stud in her nose.

"Uh, yeah," he stammers. He follows Jewel out to the floor, leaving me alone with Liberty and Mei.

"Where's Chessie tonight?" I ask Mei.

"Home. They had a performance this evening and a matinee tomorrow."

"How does she like the BSO?"

"So far, so good. Now the season is over, you have to come to one of their concerts."

I sip from the Paloma, enjoying the zing of Jarritos. "Love to."

Mei checks her watch. "All right, kiddies. I'm heading back to the hotel. Chessie and I have a FaceTime date."

She pats my arm on the way out. I'm alone with the Liberty for the first time in weeks and look around for an exit.

"Hey." I side-eye her warily. She grimaces, tossing her red ponytail over her shoulder. "Just wanted to say I'm going to miss you, too. Not in the way you think. You're a positive influence in the office. You have a knack for bringing out the best in people and for making them feel good. The Red Hawks media team is lucky to have you."

I give a terse nod. "Thanks. I appreciate it."

"You're not leaving because of me, are you?" she asks, a desperate edge to her voice. "Because I swear, I'm never going to bother you again. I was a total bitch and I really don't have an excuse. Stupid jealousy on my part."

"No, Liberty," I assure her. "Nothing to do with you."

She studies my face, maybe looking for any hint of a lie, but she won't find one. We go back to silently watching the crowd. I laugh at Dante doing some strange fish-like move that has the other women in stitches. Weird flex, but okay.

The smell of peaches wafts above the alcohol and sweat. I know it's Palmer before she even speaks, and my heart leaps into my throat. I take a drink to try to force it back into position.

"Hi, Liberty," she says, resting her hands on the back of Dante's vacated chair. She swings her eyes to me. "I'm glad you decided to come out."

"I'm leaving soon," I say, not holding her gaze. I can't. I'll lose myself in those eyes and I can't keep torturing myself over something that won't work, not in the long run.

Liberty looks between the two of us and gets up. "I need a refill. Get anyone anything?"

Palmer and I decline, and she leaves us alone. "Are you not having a good time?" Palmer asks.

"I only came for Dante and I think he's found someone prettier to hang with." I gesture to the dance floor, where he and Jewel are dancing close to one another.

Palmer grins. "She's had a bit of a crush on him."

"Think the feeling's mutual," I chuckle.

"So," Palmer says. "I was trying to tell some lacrosse jokes, but they wouldn't stick. Thought I'd see if you'd scoop them up."

I bite back a groan. "Those are terrible, Palmer."

She throws her head back and laughs. "No worse than the one you told me the first night we met. Just returning the favor."

I stare into my drink until I muster the courage to look at her. She's as beautiful as ever. I swallow hard. "I can't do this, Palmer."

"Do what?" she moves closer.

"Play this game with you anymore," I say.

"It's not a game, Charlie," she stares at me in earnest. "Not to me. Not anymore."

"See that's the thing, Palmer." My hand twitches to touch her, but I fold it into a fist because I know I'd never be able to let her go if I did. And I have to let her go. She has the power to destroy me worse than Angela ever did, and if the hurt I have now is any indication, the pain it will cost me to lose her later on would be nuclear.

"It was never a game for me," I finish. "Not really. Everything I said, I meant. Everything I felt was real. But when it came down to it, you couldn't believe in that. You didn't believe in me. You said yourself your family would never buy we were a real couple because I'm not someone who would fit in with their lifestyle."

"I was wrong," she says, the strobe from the dance floor glinting off the sheen in her eyes.

There's no humor in my laugh. "Except you weren't. It was made plain to me that day."

I run my hand through my hair. "I let someone devastate me once before. I can't do it again. I'm sorry."

She pushes herself up from the chair she is leaning on. Her

expression hardens as she rolls her shoulders back and lifts her chin. "You're a fucking coward, Carlos Salinas. It took everything in me to come over here and lay my heart out on the table to you. I risked the pain because, as scared as I was to have you reject me, I was more scared to go through the rest of my life wondering if things might have been different if I told you I loved you. And I love you, Charlie. But if you don't have the guts to take a chance on us, then I guess there really is nothing else to say."

I inhale sharply, a scramble of words stuck in my chest, eating all of the oxygen in my lungs. Palmer walks away from me, taking away her peaches, her eyes, her heart—her love.

Stop being a coward.

You're a fucking coward, Carlos Salinas.

I twist my head and catch Palmer stop at the table where Tisha and her husband sit with Vera. She says something to them and leaves. Three sets of eyes look my way, at least two of them with murder in their gaze. The third has more of a "You're an idiot" declaration in them.

What the fuck am I doing? I'm letting the woman I love walk out because I am a damn coward.

Palmer moves quickly through the crowd to the exit. Abandoning my drink, I hurry off in that direction, trying to keep her pink-streaked hair in sight, pushing through groups of clubgoers with muttered apologies. I lose her when she goes through the door and hurry to catch up.

Outside, I look left and right, but I don't see her. Where could she have gone? My chest tightens, my breaths coming out in short pants. I have to find her.

"Charlie?"

I spin and there she is leaning against the wall with her phone in her hand. My shoulders sag in relief. She walks toward me, head cocked. Her tattoo is on full display, her smooth white shoulders aglow in the fluorescents of the building signs. Her amazing, island-like eyes stare at me, shiny and bemused. Her lips part on an inhale and I dive in. I take her face in my hands and press my mouth against hers. My tongue nudges the seam of her lips and she opens for me with a hum. I kiss her and kiss her, like she is the air I need to survive. Because she is. She is everything I need. Everyone and everything around us fades away, and it's only her, in my arms, in my heart.

A few catcalls break through the bubble around us, and reluctantly, I pull away. "Palmer. I love you. More than anything and anyone I have ever loved. You're right—I've been a cowardly jackass and if you'll give me another chance, I will spend the rest of my life making it up to you. Please say you'll give me a chance."

Her lips slowly curve into a sweet, tender smile. "Okay."

My eyes close in relief. I touch my forehead to hers. "Okay? This is it, then. You and me. No more games. No more lessons."

"I kind of liked my lessons." She looks up at me with a wicked gleam in her eyes. "I feel there's so much more you can teach me."

I grunt. "There's much we can learn together, young grasshopper."

"Yeah?"

"Yeah," I say. "How about our next lesson involves how to live happily-ever-after together?"

"I'd like that," she sighs. "But first, why don't you show me how to kiss the love of your life?"

"Now that's a lesson I'm happy to teach over and over."

acknowledgments

Writing can be a solitary existence, but it's far from a lonely one when you have the right people behind you! Huge thanks to my writing partners-in-crime, JL Lora, Laralyn Doran, and Shadow Leitner, for all the advice and encouragement. I don't know what I'd do without my Damned Mob of Scribbling Women!

I'd also like to thank Christiana from Concepts by Canea for the amazing cover work. Can't wait to see the rest of the series! Also, thanks to Jenn Lockwood for the beta read (and patience).

Thank you to Katie Wilson for helping manage my Facebook page and making me sound funny! You gave me the time I needed to put words on the page.

And last but never, ever least, love and kisses to my awesome husband and kids. I love you guys! None of this would mean anything without you there cheering me on every day, even when it means dinner is fend-for-yourselves. Special shoutout to Mr. Croc—every married writer should be so lucky to have someone to rub their tired arms, make sure their cocktail glass or water bottle (depending on the need) is always full, and to constantly ask the question, "Shouldn't you be writing?" You're my inspiration and the only reason I know happily-ever-after really does exist. Elephant Shoes!

about the author

Cate Tayler is a beach baby, born and raised on the Connecticut coastline. She met the love of her life while serving in the US Air Force, and after extensive overseas travel, they are now raising their four children and two rescue pups in the wild suburbs of Maryland. When she's not living her own happily-ever-after, she's creating them in her small-town romances. In addition to writing, her passions include cooking (not baking!), everything 80s, sappy Hallmark movies, the Hershey Bears, and the Miami Dolphins. You can connect with her online at CateTayler.com.

also by cate tayler